A LORD OR A LIAR (ONLY FOR LOVE BOOK 2)

A REGENCY ROMANCE

ROSE PEARSON

A LORD OR A LIAR

PROLOGUE

"*A*nd where are you going?"

Miss Bridget Wynch barely threw a glance at her mother.

"I am going out." She waved one hand vaguely behind her. "I have my maid with me."

She waited for the moment, wondering if her mother would ask her precisely where she was going, or state that it was improper for her to do so, but no remark came. Stifling a sigh, Bridget turned towards the door, comprehending that, yet again, she was of little distinction to her mother, the Viscountess Culpepper, far less important than her sister, Sophia, who was the middle sister. A sister who was only older than her by one year, but who took up a great deal more of her mother's time, given just how beautiful she was. To Lady Culpepper's eye, Bridget appeared not to have developed the same beauty as Sophia. How often she had looked in the mirror, considering herself, wishing that Lady Culpepper would look upon her with the same fondness! Certainly, she was not plain, but even to her own eyes, she had not been blessed with the same sparkling beauty which her sister Sophia so gleefully possessed. She did not have the bright twinkling eyes, the laughing smile, the rosy cheeks. No, she had pale features, pale blue eyes that lacked any sort of vivacity, and a smile that, while warm, did not make gentlemen pause in their steps, simply so that they might look at her.

Unfortunately, Sophia was all too aware of her own beauty *and* of her mother's preference, doing all that she could to ignore Bridget on every occasion while pushing herself forward at every opportunity. Thus, Bridget had become accustomed to stepping into the shadows and allowing Sophia to shine brightly instead. After all, what would be the good of pushing herself forward if no one was to look at her?

Aware of the heaviness in her soul, Bridget slipped on her bonnet and stepped outside. Tilting her head towards the sky for a moment, she hastily dropped it again, glad that it was a fine day, but wary of allowing the sun to press any freckles into her skin. Such things would detract all the more from the little beauty she had. Making certain that the ribbons of her bonnet were tied under her chin, Bridget made her way directly to the carriage and paused, looking up at the coachman.

"To Dove Street. My usual place." The coachman said very little, giving her a small nod. He had taken her there on various occasions already and knew precisely which place she meant. "And as quickly as you can, if you please. I do not want to be tardy."

With the aid of a footman, Bridget climbed inside, and the carriage door was shut behind her. Ignoring the presence of her maid, Bridget laid her head back, closing her eyes and telling herself to concentrate her thoughts on the orphanage, rather than on how little her mother considered her. That was her one blessing, for Lady Culpepper showed very little interest in where she was, her father certainly did not care, and her sister disregarded everything Bridget did or said. Whether or not any of them would approve of her giving her time to those less fortunate, Bridget did not know, but nor did she care. Ever since she had come to London some years ago with her eldest sister – a sister who was now married and contented - Bridget had taken her responsibilities seriously, seeing the destitution and the hardship which clung to the darker streets of London. She had listened to the Parson as he had spoken on generosity of spirit, as well as of heart, believing now that the instruction to care for those less fortunate was not an optional one.

Thus, during her time in London when she was not herself out in society, Bridget had spent many hours in the local orphanage. It was not a practice she was about to give up simply because this Season was her own Come Out and, she considered, in some sense, that this was where she felt most at ease. She was not inclined towards the *ton* in any way, aware that she was being pushed to the very bottom of society's view simply because she did not bear the same beauty as her sister. At the orphanage, she was able to forget all about Sophia, and about the requirements and expectations which came with being a supposedly eligible young lady. It was a place where she felt as though she had some worth, herself. It was also a reminder to her that her struggles were not as significant as those of others, and an opportunity to recall just how much she possessed in this world – which, as the carriage made its way there, Bridget once more brought to mind.

Pushing away the pain which came from being entirely ignored by her mother, Bridget took a deep breath and found herself smiling. Regardless of the requirement to find herself a husband this Season, she was determined to visit the orphanage as much as she had done in previous years. After all, this would be Sophia's second Season and thus, the urge for *her* to marry was surely greater than the pressure on Bridget herself! Mayhap once Sophia was wed, her mother would focus a little more on Bridget and *her* requirement to marry also.

But even then, even if Lady Culpepper fixed her attention on Bridget, she silently swore that she would not abandon those in the orphanage to concentrate instead on her own pleasures. No, the orphanage and those within it would remain important to her, and if any gentleman wished to pursue her, then they would pursue her with a full understanding of what she gave her time to.

I will not marry a self-interested gentleman.

Nodding to herself, Bridget drew in a long breath, her smile flattening. She was quite determined not to marry a gentleman who had even the smallest hint of selfishness about him. Should he mock her, should he tease her for giving her time to such an endeavor, then she would immediately consider him unworthy. Smiling softly to herself, Bridget recalled how she and her friends had determined to marry for love. Thus far this Season, Lady Cassandra had found herself quite in love with a gentleman who loved her also - a gentleman of great worth. Might she hope for her own happiness to follow?

"Whoa, there!"

Bridget's soft smile shattered as the carriage swerved sharply to one side, throwing her across the carriage seat. She caught her breath, scrabbling at the strap as she attempted to right herself, only for the coachman to begin exclaiming furiously as the carriage came to a standstill.

"Whatever has happened?"

Her voice was a little weak as she released the strap, her hand going to her heart instead.

"Are you quite all right, Miss Wynch?" The white-faced maid reached to grasp Bridget's hand. "Are you injured?"

Managing a brief smile, Bridget nodded.

"I am quite all right." Moving to the side of the carriage, she looked out the window, only to see a lady shouting furiously from the window of *her* carriage. With green, flashing eyes, a tight jaw, and a furious red growing in her cheeks, she appeared to be the very epitome of anger. "Good gracious!"

Without even considering what she was doing, Bridget pushed the door open, intending to step out of the carriage - much to the horror of her maid, who immediately tried to tug Bridget back again.

"Miss Wynch, you must not!"

"I must." Bridget spoke with a firmness that brooked no argument, and she felt the maid's hand release her own as she stepped out, jumping lightly to the road and putting both hands on her hips as the lady in question continued to shout at Bridget's coachman. "Whatever happened here?"

The shouting quietened a little as both her own coachman and the red-faced lady turned to look at her.

"Forgive me, Miss Wynch."

Her coachman immediately began to apologize, but Bridget silenced him with a wave of her hand.

"I am certain that you were not at fault, Andrews." Her eyebrows lifted as the lady in the carriage scowled at her. "You have been an excellent coachman for many years. I cannot imagine now that the reason I was flung from one side of my carriage to the other is because of you."

So saying, she lifted an eyebrow in the lady's direction,

and the green-eyed woman simply narrowed her eyes back at her.

"Am I to understand it that *my* coachman is to be blamed for this?"

The lady's harsh tones matched the anger burning across her features, but Bridget was not about to allow her obvious anger to push Bridget aside.

"Your coachman was reckless! The streets may be quieter, but that does not mean he can drive without thinking or noticing anyone else, or that you should be encouraging him to push the horses forward – yes, I saw you doing that very thing! What you *should* be asking is whether or not my lady is in any way injured!"

The angry tones of her coachman surprised Bridget, but she was glad of his words, seemingly unafraid to sharpen his tone towards a lady who was much higher in rank than he. She lifted an eyebrow in the lady's direction, seeing her open her mouth to defend what she had been doing. Upon Bridget catching her eye, however, the green-eyed lady simply snapped her mouth shut and tossed her head.

"I beg of you to be more careful." Lifting her chin, Bridget spoke with as much temerity as she could muster. "I do not much appreciate being slung from one side of my carriage to the other and, in the future, should like to be spared from such an indignity."

The lady said nothing, instead giving a sharp nod of her head and a wave of her hand to her coachman, who then picked up the reins, clicked to his horses, and continued on his way. With a small smile, Bridget nodded to her own coachman and then stepped back into the carriage. Sitting down, she pulled the door tightly closed and ignored the huge eyes of her maid, seeing just how concerned the young lady had been over Bridget's behavior.

"The lady was pushing her coachman to recklessness. Regardless of her rank, she ought not to be able to drive about as she pleases," Bridget said aloud as though she needed to confirm with the maid that what she had done was perfectly acceptable. "Let us make our way to the orphanage in the hope that he is not going in the very same direction!"

As the carriage continued to move away, Bridget could not help but think of that lady's stony face. She had appeared very disgruntled indeed – perhaps even angry - for neither she nor her coachman had even *considered* apologizing. Her lips twisted. In that regard, the lady appeared to be both arrogant and self-confident. She admired the latter but only if it did not impinge upon others.

I highly doubt that such a lady would ever come near an orphanage.

With a wry smile, she rapped on the roof and the carriage continued on toward the Dove Street orphanage.

CHAPTER ONE

"I confess I am utterly astonished."

Heath Northdale, Earl of Landon, rolled his eyes.

"Why should you be?" Tilting his head, he grinned at his friend. "Is it not the task of every gentleman to find themselves a wife?"

"Never did I think you would sound so eager." Lord Atherton frowned, a line cutting between his brows. "You are aware, I hope, that the young ladies of the *ton* are never truly as they appear. They play a part when in London, in amongst society. They pretend that they are just as amiable and just as delightful as you might wish them to be, while at the same time proving themselves to be entirely otherwise when they are not in company."

Taking this as nothing more than a cynical remark, Heath laughed.

"Goodness, such is a very displeasing thought." He grinned as his friend nodded sagely, as if imparting the wisest advice. "Surely you cannot believe that every young lady is not as she appears?"

"I certainly do." Lord Atherton lifted his chin. "Heath, mark my words, the moment you take a young lady to the altar is the moment that she will revert to her true self. You will find yourself astonished - horrified, even – over how easily you have been deceived." He waggled one finger as though Heath was nothing but a schoolboy, requiring teaching and information about the ladies of London for the very first time. "They have many tricks to make you believe in their suitability, certainly. You will find yourself captivated by them, find yourself believing that yes, they are more than suitable for you, only to then discover that their true nature is not as you believed."

"I do not believe such things." Seeing his friend pitying him, given the way that he shook his head and let out a heavy sigh, Heath could only chuckle. "I am afraid I am certainly not as cynical as you, old friend."

"Mayhap you shall be one day." Lord Atherton remarked, an air of confidence about him. "I will pray, however, that you will be one of the lucky few to find themselves easily contented with a bride who will not be as much of a disappointment as she might be. And might I also remind you to be extremely careful when it comes to making your choice?"

"Which I fully intend to be." Heath took a sip of his brandy, a little surprised at his friend's strenuous reaction. He had not expected Lord Atherton to be so filled with angst when it came to Heath's intention to wed, having assumed that his friend would be entirely supportive. Instead, he had been offered this furious reaction and encouragement *not* to do as he intended. "A gentleman cannot avoid matrimony." With a shrug, Heath looked back steadily at his friend. "I intend to find out a great deal about whichever young lady I choose – and indeed, I intend to find someone who will *not* hide her true character from me; someone who will be more than inclined to reveal her heart. I am not seeking a love match, not by any means, but I certainly hope for trueness of character and spirit which might encourage a close connection. I am certain such a young lady will not be too difficult to discover."

Lord Atherton snorted. Evidently, he believed that it would be a good deal more difficult than Heath expected, but Heath was not about to take Lord Atherton's warnings with any real seriousness. His friend clearly had concerns over the young ladies of the *ton,* and where such concerns came from, Heath did not know – but certainly he did not share those worries. Surely, with the Season already under-way, it would not be too difficult to find a suitable young lady amongst the many who were present.

"No doubt your sister will be delighted."

This made Heath wince.

"She has always been desperate for me to wed, even though she is settled with her own family now. I believe she is concerned about the family line."

Lord Atherton rolled his eyes, as though to suggest that young ladies ought not to be worried over such matters.

"And your brother?"

Heath swallowed hard, the shadows of the past threatening to swoop down upon him, guilt tearing through his heart.

"You know very well that my sister-in-law has never taken a particular inclination towards me." Taking a breath, he pushed away the menacing guilt. "Obviously, it is entirely unmerited."

Lord Atherton chuckled, lifting his brandy glass to his lips.

"Absolutely." His smile fixed for a moment as he studied

Heath. "Have you any understanding of why she has always disliked you?"

Heath considered for a moment, wondering whether his friend remembered what had taken place some five years ago.

"Yes, I know why," he replied honestly. "If you recall, she attempted to seek out my interest first but I was not inclined towards matrimony at the time, given that I had just been handed the responsibility of the title." Again, his guilt and shame reared up and Heath fought to control it. "She decided to wed my brother instead."

Shrugging, Heath looked away from his friend, fighting still to push away every last hint of conscience. Even Lord Atherton – a gentleman who had been friends with Heath for many years – did not know the truth and, certainly, Heath was not about to share it with him. Reminding himself that he had done as he had simply for the good of the family, he took a long breath.

"So the lady is frustrated with you because you would not marry her."

Lord Atherton shook his head.

Heath shrugged, dismissing that part of the conversation.

"Such things do not trouble me. If she is to dislike me, then so be it. She will no doubt dislike whichever young lady I decide to make my bride also." With a grin, he picked up his brandy glass and threw the rest back, with relish. "I should make my way to Lord Newport's ball. My search must begin at once!"

Lord Atherton lifted his eyebrows.

"You intend to begin seeking out a potential bride this very evening?"

"But of course." Heath rose to his feet. "Why should I

wait? Although I would beg of you to keep what we have spoken of to yourself. I should not want everyone in society to know of my intentions!"

Lord Atherton blinked away his confusion.

"Very well then, if you are to attend this ball, I believe I shall also." He got to his feet also, looking down somewhat sorrowfully at his now empty glass. "That brandy was exceptional."

"But the ball shall be all the more so," Heath chuckled. "This will undoubtedly be a pleasant evening. I will be paying great attention to the young ladies present but, no doubt, there will be brandy there to distract *you*."

Lord Atherton chuckled, clapping one hand onto Heath's shoulder.

"One thing I must know. Where has this desire come from? Last Season you did not so much as mention the word 'marriage'!"

A trifle embarrassed, Heath shrugged both shoulders.

"It is my duty. This last year, I have become increasingly aware that there is no continuing line." Turning, he made his way to the door, still speaking as he went. "Should the worst happen, then it would be my twin brother who would take the title, and that situation would not be a pleasant one. He may have changed somewhat, but not enough to prove to me that he would be able to bear the title responsibly."

"That is because your brother is reckless, foolish, and irresponsible." The liquor had clearly loosened Lord Atherton's tongue, and while Heath frowned, he did not immediately disagree. "Is he to be in London this Season?"

Heath shook his head.

"No, he is to stay at the small estate my father bequeathed to him upon his death. Apparently, there are to be some improvements undertaken and this spring and summer is when they are to be done. Thus, my brother intends to remain where he is for the moment – he and his wife both."

Surprise slowly edged itself across Lord Atherton's expression.

"Then mayhap he is not as irresponsible as I stated." He spoke slowly, a good deal more cautiously than before. "Has gaining the estate changed him somewhat?"

"A little," Heath acknowledged, "but not enough where I would be comfortable considering him as the next Earl of Landon. That being said, I am hopeful it will be a prolonged change that will only continue to grow."

His heart sank as he made such remarks to Lord Atherton about his twin brother, sorrowful over his brother's lack of maturity and responsibility. No, it would be best for Heath to find his own bride and, thereafter, produce the heir required. He would be able to train him in all that was necessary, resting in the assurance that the title would pass on favorably to a man who would treat it with as much dignity and as much gravitas as was required. For the moment, his brother was simply not a viable alternative.

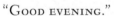

"Good evening."

The evening was not going as well as Heath had expected. Thus far, his time in the ballroom had been filled with conversation and dancing with many young ladies, but he was slowly being somewhat overcome by the sheer number who were introduced to him. He could not draw breath, and had fought back the expectation of signing dance cards for fear he would give them all away much too soon. It was as though the young ladies of London had over-heard his conversation with Lord Atherton in White's and were now crowding around him, like a cloud of billowing smoke, so that he lost himself in the middle of them. There were so many faces, so many smiles, so many shining eyes. He could not even remember the name of the last young lady he had been introduced to!

His gaze went to Lord Atherton. The gentleman was talking to a young lady and her mother – but as Heath watched, he caught Lord Atherton's gesture towards him. Lord Atherton's grin followed as the young lady's eyes went wide, making him catch his breath in horror.

With a groan, he passed one hand over his eyes, his heart sinking low. Lord Atherton had clearly allowed liquor to loosen his tongue even more, and was now busy informing those present this evening that Lord Landon was seeking a bride for himself, and intended to wed very soon indeed. Little wonder Heath had found himself so surrounded!

Taking a deep breath, Heath turned his head, realizing that the young lady he had been speaking to had been talking for so long, she had not even seemed to notice that he had not been paying attention. Forcing a smile and trying desperately to work out a manner in which he might escape, Heath let his gaze dance about the room. His stomach knotted, a flood of anger rushing through his frame, only for it to fade away as Lord Atherton chuckled and waved one hand in Heath's direction for what was the second time.

I should never have said a word to him.

The gentleman was foolish, certainly, but they had been friends for so long, he should have known not to speak so in front of a gentleman who was well-known for offering his opinions and thoughts much too freely. All the same, Heath now needed to silence his friend just as soon as he was able.

"Pray excuse me, I see my friend requires my presence for a moment."

No doubt it was a little rude for him to step away in such an abrupt manner, but Heath had no intention of lingering, nor furthering his conversation with the young lady whose name he could not recall. This was no way to find a bride! Not when they were all pushing him forward, begging him to look at them, to glance at them, to speak with them. It would be as Lord Atherton had said. They would push themselves forward, pretending to be just as perfect as he might require, but he would not truly get to know their character. Each lady would be just as they had been trained to be - proper, genteel, amiable, able to sing, dance, play the pianoforte or paint beautiful scenes. They might speak of their enjoyment in reading quietly during the evening, of enjoying peaceful walks in the countryside - but he would not know their true nature. They would speak as they had been directed, all in the hope of making a suitable match.

Then how am I to find a suitable young lady if I cannot truly know their character until we are wed?

Stopping next to Lord Atherton, he settled one hand on his shoulder for a moment, leaning in and interrupting the gentleman's conversation in the most direct manner.

"You do recall that what I said to you was meant to be kept rather private, do you not?"

Lord Atherton turned his head sharply, his smile dissolving, his eyes clearing, and Heath merely arched one eyebrow before continuing on his way across the ballroom. Hopefully, that would be the end of Lord Atherton's voice whispering into the ears of the many young ladies present here... but the damage was already done.

Moving to the edge of the ballroom, Heath found a quiet place amongst the shadows and hid there. Leaning back, he rested his head against the wall and let out a rush of breath, closing his eyes as he did so.

A slight sound caught his attention. His eyes flew open, and he twisted his head side to side, seeking the source of the sound, only to catch sight of a young lady. She was not standing by the wall near him, but sitting in a chair only a short distance away. There appeared to be nobody with her. Her head was steadfastly turned in the opposite direction, but Heath could still see the hint of a smile pulling at one corner of her mouth. Had she been laughing at him?

His face flushed and Heath cleared his throat, feeling the need to say something to explain himself, even though he did not know the young lady.

"I am sure you can understand a gentleman being required to catch his breath." Even to himself, his tone sounded brusque, and he winced. "I would be obliged to you if you did not indicate to anyone else that I am standing here at present."

"Certainly, my Lord." The young lady said nothing more, keeping her head turned away. He could only see her profile, and that in itself was half hidden in shadow. A strange desire to see her face began to grow within him, but he threw that aside quickly enough. She was clearly unchaperoned, and it would not be wise for him to speak to her when she was in such a position. Quite why she was unchaperoned he could not imagine, although after a moment of consideration, he wondered if it was because she might be something of a wallflower. "My mother will return very soon." The lady spoke as though she understood his thoughts. "If you are wondering why there is no one here but myself, it is simply because my mother insisted on introducing my sister to her particular gentleman."

"And you are not to be introduced?"

This time, the young lady *did* turn her face towards him. Brown curls framed her face, with a great heap pulled to the very back. She had rosebud lips, a gentle, sloping nose, and a softness in her expression that seemed to draw him in. Her eyes met his, a rueful smile on her lips and a slight flicker of sadness in those light blue eyes.

"I am afraid not."

Her expression did not alter, and she said nothing further, leaving Heath to deduce how she truly felt about being so excluded. Finding himself a little sorry for her, he smiled when she again turned her head in his direction.

"It is most improper to introduce oneself, but I shall do so regardless." He inclined his head, relief coming with the realization that *this* young lady would not have heard anything about his desire to seek a bride, not if she had been sitting here alone. With her, he could speak quite freely. "I am the Earl of Landon."

The young lady blinked, her eyes widening a little before she inclined her head, rather than standing to curtsey.

"I am Miss Wynch, and my father is the Viscount Culpepper." She threw out one hand in the direction of the other guests, her nose wrinkling a little – although this was swiftly smoothed away. "As I have said, my mother is, at present, taking my sister, Miss Sophia Wynch, to meet a gentleman of interest, otherwise I would introduce them to you also."

Her shoulders lifted in a small shrug and Heath smiled, finding himself rather taken with the young lady. Thus far, this Miss Wynch appeared to be very amiable and yet presented herself without any desire to offer a particular façade to him. She spoke just as things were, telling him the truth about her situation without any ambiguity. She might have pretended that she was waiting for her mother to bring back a suitable gentleman for her, or that she was fatigued after her many, many dances and had sought to escape for a short while, but instead, she had chosen to be honest, and Heath considered it most refreshing.

"And are you to dance this evening?"

It was perhaps a somewhat foolish thing to ask, given that they had not been properly introduced, but Heath considered that, given the number of guests this evening, most would assume they had been introduced properly. The desire to dance with her, to continue their conversation, was strong, and he smiled at the way her eyes flared wide. Had she not expected such a thing?

"I am."

Miss Wynch made no attempt to remove herself from her chair, but simply held his gaze, one eyebrow slightly arched as though she could not quite believe that he was asking her to dance with him.

"Would you like to stand up with me? If you have some dances still available, of course." Given her astonishment, Heath did not want to take for granted the fact that she would be willing to dance with him, but it was with great relief that he saw how eagerly she nodded. "I should probably find someone to make certain that we are introduced properly."

A quiet laugh came from the lady and a flood of surprise rushed through him – not only from her laugh but also from how warm her expression became when she smiled.

"I would not worry yourself, Lord Landon. I do not

think that anyone will even question whether or not we have been introduced. My mother may be a little surprised, but she will assume that one of my acquaintances has introduced us.... if she even notices at all! Pray, do not overly concern yourself. I am not of particular importance to anyone."

This last remark was said quite plainly, without any seeming distress or batting of her eyelashes, nor seeking to garner his sympathy. All the same, Heath did not like to hear her say such a thing, wondering why her mother overlooked her so.

"Then you shall be of importance to me, Miss Wynch."

Where such a remark had come from, he was a little uncertain, but it was with a great rush of pleasure that he saw Miss Wynch flush red as she smiled at him.

"You are very kind, Lord Landon."

So saying, she rose to her feet and handed him her dance card, which Heath took at once, choosing two of the remaining dances which were in quick succession of each other. He was glad to do so, and even more delighted to see the smile of pure happiness which lingered on Miss Wynch's face.

"I look forward to dancing with you, Miss Wynch."

"As do I with you."

Their eyes met for a moment, and a sudden fluttery sensation spilled through Heath's stomach. It was only when his gaze snagged on Lord Atherton, seeing him beginning to approach, that he forced himself to step away from Miss Wynch. What he did not want was for his friends to come and interrupt the conversation, perhaps then going on to spread another rumor about Heath's interest in the young lady – although perhaps him having claimed two dances would create that, anyway. Well, it was done now, and he would not regret it.

"Until later this evening, Miss Wynch."

With a small inclination of his head, he stepped away from her. As he walked, he could not help but glance over his shoulder, smiling to himself as he saw her looking down at her dance card, as though she could not quite believe that she had been offered two dances. He did not feel proud, but simply pleased that a young lady, who appeared to linger somewhat in the shadow of her sister, was now going to be able to step out into the light. A light, he considered, which she wholeheartedly deserved.

CHAPTER TWO

"And thus, it seems we have found our first success."

Lady Yardley's smile ran around the room before her gaze lingered fondly on her cousin.

"Lady Cassandra and Lord Sherbourne have found happiness together. We look forward to hearing news of their betrothal once her father responds with his acceptance."

"Which I am certain he will give without hesitation," Lady Cassandra murmured, her cheeks rather bright, but her smile evidence of the love she had found with Lord Sherbourne.

Bridget sighed softly to herself, elated for her friend and yet, at the same time, wishing desperately that she too would be able to find something as wonderful as the love that Lady Cassandra had discovered with Lord Sherbourne. That was what they had all promised to each other, swearing that they would assist one another in their quest for a love match. Lady Cassandra had found hers, but the rest of them were still in the midst of their searches.

"I have not forgotten my promise to the rest of you,

however." Lady Cassandra looked around the room, her gaze lingering on Bridget for a moment, as though she had heard her thought. "I recall how we swore that we would assist one another in our search for a love match. Simply because I have found happiness does not mean that I will forget the rest of you. I intend to do all I can to be of assistance, to help guide you in much the same way that Lady Yardley and even Lord Sherbourne himself have guided me."

Bridget smiled back at her friends. Lady Cassandra was one of the kindest young ladies of her acquaintance, and she knew that her words were genuinely meant.

"As do I also." Lady Yardley's smile softened. "Yes, my cousin has found her happy connection, but I will not turn my back on the rest of you. 'The London Ledger' will continue to be written and, as has been done with Lady Cassandra, you are all welcome to use it to seek out a true-hearted fellow for yourself."

Bridget caught the edge of her lip with her teeth, frowning for a moment as she cast her gaze down to the floor. Yes, Lady Cassandra had used 'The London Ledger' – the publication in which Lady Yardley wrote about society matters - to make certain that one gentleman was as true as he said he was, but Bridget herself was unsure how she might use it.

Surely, my challenge is to find a gentleman in the first place!

The thought made her smile ruefully, shaking her head as she lifted her gaze back to the others in the room. She caught Lady Yardley smiling at her, making Bridget wonder if somehow, the lady knew what she had been thinking.

"Finding a love match may take some time, but it will be worthwhile." Lady Yardley continued to look in Bridget's direction as she spoke as if talking directly to her. "I would encourage you to take as much time as you can in getting to know the gentlemen of the *ton*, and especially any who shows you particular attention." Lady Yardley spread out both hands. "Have any of you a new acquaintance? A gentleman of interest? I ask, not so I might write about them in the Ledger, but purely out of interest to know which gentlemen are speaking with you. There may be some I will know instantly to warn you away from."

Immediately, Bridget's thoughts turned to the gentleman who had spoken to her last evening, the gentleman who had been so very kind as to first notice her, and thereafter give her not one, but two dances. She smiled to herself, recalling her mother's astonishment to see her standing up with such a fine fellow. He had seemed very pleasant with good conversation and she, in turn, had spoken with more openness than she had expected or intended. In addition to all of this, Lord Landon was certainly very handsome, with his dark hair, swirling brown eyes, broad smile, and easy manner - but that did not mean that he intended to pay her any particular attention. She had been introduced to a good many gentlemen, and none of them as yet had ever sought her specific company. None had suggested a walk in the park or a ride in their carriage. Yes, there had been some gentleman callers, but there had been very few who lingered, and none who had called again. Could she expect anything more from Lord Landon?

Her stomach dropped, her smile dying away. If she were to be honest, what was most likely to happen would be that Lord Landon would behave as the other gentlemen had. He might dance with her, might speak to her on occasion, but Bridget could not expect anything more. She was a wallflower, she reminded herself.

"You were speaking and dancing with a new gentleman last evening, were you not, Bridget?"

Miss Millington looked over at her, smiling gently as Bridget's face immediately warmed.

"I was, but I do not think I need to consider him with any real interest."

Nonchalantly, she tried to shrug, aware of just how much she desired to be in his company again.

"Who was he?" It was Lady Almeria who turned to speak to Bridget, her eyes clear with interest. "As yet, I do not think I have seen you blush over any gentleman!" This only caused Bridget's face to heat all the more, and she dropped her gaze to her clasped hands, wishing that Miss Millington had not spoken so. While she was determined within herself, she was also rather quiet, not often speaking of her feelings, wishes, and desires. It was the very antithesis of her character to be asked such a question, with the expectation being that she would answer. "If you do not wish to say, we will not press you." Lady Almeria smiled warmly, perhaps seeing Bridget's discomfiture in her manner. "Although I would also encourage you by saying that there is nothing to be embarrassed about."

"No, there is not," Lady Cassandra added. "This is what we all seek, is it not? We each hope for the one gentleman who will have a heart filled with love for us – and who we will love in return. And that love starts with a flicker of interest."

"I am certainly not interested in him." Her response was so sharp that even Bridget caught her breath. "I apologize." Taking a breath, she kept her tone more measured. "Please do not think that I have any interest in any specific gentleman. Lord Landon was very kind to stand up with me. Indeed, he and I danced twice, and yes, I do think well of him because of that kindness, but that is all."

She looked around the room, taking in the slightly widened eyes and lifted eyebrows on each of her friend's faces. They had not expected her to speak so, and now she was somewhat embarrassed.

"Lord Landon." Lady Yardley repeated the name slowly, her brow furrowing slightly. "There is nothing about him that comes to mind... which is of course an excellent thing, for it means that there is no disagreeable trait within him that is well known to everyone! I will do some further searching, of course."

She smiled warmly and Bridget offered a nod in return, wishing Lord Landon's name had not been mentioned. Had they not heard her say that she had no interest in him?

"Well, if he *does* pay you any further attention, you know that we will all be eager to assist you." Miss Madeley tilted her head, her expression gentle. "And do not fear being open with us. We must all be so, if we are to be of aid to each other."

Bridget hesitated, pressing her lips together.

"Whilst the latter is so – and I thank you for it - I do not think that any further deliberations will be required." With the lift of her shoulder, she began to explain, seeing Lady Yardley look across at her with a steady gaze. "Lord Landon is clearly a well-established gentleman within society. He carries a high title, possesses a good deal of wealth, and can have as many acquaintances as he wishes. I, on the other hand, am very much inclined towards standing at the side of the room, draped in shadow as my sister is given prominence." She lifted one shoulder, trying to disguise the terrible sadness which suddenly gripped her heart. "Lord Landon may be the very best of gentlemen, Lady Yardley, but I have no expectation that he will offer me any particular attention, not when he could have the interest of any young lady he wishes for."

Silence ran around the room and Bridget immediately dropped her head, her embarrassment beginning to creep over her again. She had not intended to speak so bluntly or garner any sort of sympathy for herself, but only to express the truth of the situation, as far as she saw it.

"There is no reason for your mother to be pushing your sister forward and keeping you back." Miss Millington spoke a little sharply, her eyes slightly narrowed, as though she were doing her best to express to Bridget her displeasure whilst, at the same time, making certain not to speak poorly of Lady Culpepper. "You are just as beautiful, just as lovely, and just as suitable a bride for a gentleman as Sophia."

At this, tears began to burn in the corners of Bridget's eyes.

"You are very kind."

"It is not kindness which makes me speak so." Miss Millington fixed her with a hard look. "I say such things because they are entirely true. You may have a quieter disposition than Sophia and yes, she may be a year older than you, but that does not mean that you should be as forgotten as you are."

"I quite agree."

Lady Yardley's murmur was met with nods and exclamations of agreement from the rest of Bridget's friends. Looking around, Bridget swallowed hard as the tears lodged in her throat, her heart swelling a little, grateful to them for their encouragement.

"And that means you should expect someone such as Lord Landon to be interested in you, and in furthering your connection." Lady Elizabeth added as Bridget's heart lurched with a sudden, fierce hope. "Therefore, if you find yourself in his company again, if you find him seeking you out for a dance and the like, then pray do not hold yourself back from him, believing someone else will capture his attention first when *you* are the one who has done so!"

Bridget smiled, managing to push back the threat of tears.

"Very well. If Lord Landon shows me even the slightest bit of interest, then I promise I will tell you, and will consider 'The London Ledger' also." Looking again around the room, she smiled at each of her friends in turn. "Only pray that he is as he appears to be – an amiable, genteel, kind-hearted gentleman who, one day, I might be able to trust with my heart."

"And are you dancing this evening?"

Bridget turned quickly as a voice came to her over her shoulder. She had been standing to the side of the ballroom once more, although Miss Millington had come to be in company with her for a short while. Now, however, Miss Millington was dancing and, as had been Bridget's expectation, her mother had left Bridget alone whilst she had taken Sophia through the crowd, expecting to have her dance card filled by the time they returned.

"How did you know where to find me?" Bridget tried to ignore the quickening of her pulse as he smiled at her. "This ballroom is very busy indeed!"

Lord Landon chuckled.

"I did wonder where I might find you, but then I recalled the last time we were conversing together. Thus, I promenaded around the room at the edge until I discovered you." His eyes twinkled as he grinned. "But I do not like to see you so in the shadow. I feel it my duty to bring you out into the light."

Upon hearing this, Bridget flushed and did not know where to look. The fact that he had come deliberately to seek her out, as well as the fact that he was being so complimentary, meant that her cheeks were now burning.

"Thank you, Lord Landon. You are very kind."

She had never received such attention from any gentleman before. Was Lord Landon truly eager for her company? Or did he treat all young ladies so, because of the kindness so clearly within him?

"You have not answered my question, Miss Wynch."

Bridget finally met his eyes again.

"My Lord?"

He grinned at her.

"Are you dancing this evening?"

"If someone should ask me, then yes, I would."

Bridget flashed him a smile as he held out his hand towards her.

"I believe I am asking, Miss Wynch." The grin on his face sent a flash into his dark brown eyes as she handed him the card, her stomach roiling with something akin to nervous excitement. Her fingers twisted together as she clasped her hands tightly. Lord Landon's eyes moved over the dance card, looking at the dances which still were to be danced this evening. Thus far, Bridget had stepped out for none of them, which was not an unusual occurrence by any means. "Might I ask," Lord Landon lifted his head. "Are you permitted to waltz?" The astonishment of such a question and what it could mean sent Bridget into a state of rapturous excitement. Her heart began to pound furiously, her skin prickling, her hair pushing away from her skin, and all she could do was nod. Lord Landon dropped his head again. "Capital." He signed his name at her waltz and then handed the dance card back again. Her gaze dropped to it, and she caught her breath, realizing now that she was again to stand up with him twice – which was, in fact, overwhelming just in itself! But she was not only to stand up with him for the quadrille, but also the waltz. Was she truly to be so favored? "Does this satisfy you?"

Curling her fingers into a tight fist, Bridget forced herself to answer in a calm manner rather than with any exultant jubilation.

"That is more than delightful." She managed to smile. "It is more than I expected."

Lord Landon smiled back at her and, with a small bow, excused himself, telling her that he hoped a good many other gentlemen would come to dance with her also. Bridget watched him walk away, her heart filled with a happiness that she had never before experienced. Whether or not Lord Landon felt anything for her, she considered him to be most excellent gentleman. In fact, she considered, tilting her head, she was becoming a little afraid that, were she not careful. she would find herself entirely in love with him – and to love a gentleman who did not love her in return would surely be a most painful thing.

But all the same, her gaze continued to follow the retreating figure of Lord Landon. Try as she might, she could not help but respond to him, and the thought of soon being in his arms was the most wonderful idea imaginable.

CHAPTER THREE

"I very much enjoyed dancing the waltz with you."

The truth was, Heath had delighted in the opportunity to stand up with a young lady who did not look at him with bright shining eyes and a fixed smile as she attempted to make herself obvious in her delight. Miss Wynch had been a joy, for she danced well, spoke just as easily, and did not attempt to push herself further into his considerations in any way - and to Heath, such things were greatly enamoring. Unfortunately for her, she was also about to garner a good many fierce looks and angry glances from the other young ladies who had not been able to stand up with him for the waltz. Sighing inwardly, Heath wondered if he ought to warn her about it.

"You were very kind to ask me. I do not think I have ever danced the waltz before."

Looking down in surprise, Heath patted her hand lightly as she threaded it through his arm.

"Then might I say, you danced it very well. You showed not even a hint of nervousness. I am all the more in admiration of you."

Miss Wynch chuckled, her eyes twinkling as she glanced back at him.

"But surely you know that every young lady in London is encouraged to hide their feelings as best they can? I confess to you that I was rather terrified of dancing it with you."

"Then I am even more impressed." Silently thinking to himself that this did, in fact, encourage him to consider Miss Wynch when it came to the possibility of matrimony, Heath's smile grew. Certainly, her father was not as highly titled as his family might expect, but such things did not matter to him a great deal. If Miss Wynch was as much of a delight as she appeared to be, then he would be foolish not to consider her. "Might l call upon you tomorrow, Miss Wynch?"

He spoke rather hurriedly, the idea having only just come to him, but found that his heart was settled on the thought of calling on her, of spending a little more time in her company. She glanced at him at once, her eyes rather wide.

"You – you wish to call upon me?" Blinking, she paused for a moment. "I did not ever expect –"

"If you are much too busy with other callers, then I quite understand." Something heavy dropped into the pit of Heath's stomach. "I should expect a young lady such as yourself is taken up by many visitors."

Much to his surprise, Miss Wynch let out a soft laugh, shaking her head as she did so.

"No, Lord Landon, you mistake me." The smile she directed at him was a little sad. "It is not that I am already taken up with anyone, or have too many visitors. It is only that I have another engagement."

"With another gentleman?" The question was out of his

mouth before Heath could prevent it from springing forth. Embarrassed, he dropped his head and ran one hand over his face. "Forgive me, your business is your own. I should not be questioning you about anything."

Miss Wynch squeezed his arm lightly.

"Do not be concerned, I do not mind. My engagement is not with any particular gentleman. Therefore, I should be glad if you would call upon me again at your earliest convenience, after tomorrow. I can assure you that I have no other gentlemen seeking to come to call."

When Heath looked at her, he saw that she was now the one wincing, clearly embarrassed that she had spoken so, mayhap feeling just as uncertain and as awkward as he did. Smiling, he took in a deep breath.

"Then I should be very glad to call on you in two days' time."

"That would suit me very well." A blush warmed her cheeks lightly as she smiled up at him. "I look forward to your visit."

"As do I."

WALKING through town the following day, Heath found himself rather distracted. He had stepped out that afternoon simply to enjoy a short walk, for it was an opportunity to speak with various acquaintances and have a pleasant afternoon, but his mind simply would not keep itself fixed on anything other than Miss Wynch. She was not able to meet with him that afternoon, of course, which was mayhap why his thoughts lingered on her, and what she was doing. It was none of his business, of course, but Heath could not help but wonder what a young lady such as herself might be doing.

"Landon, there you are." A gentleman stopped directly in Heath's path, and Heath caught himself just in time, having been lost in thought. Lord Atherton dropped his head, one hand scrubbing over his face as Heath exclaimed aloud, evidently struggling to bring his gaze towards Heath. "I went to your townhouse and then came here in search of you."

"Why? And why stride into my path like that?"

Lord Atherton sighed.

"Because I am heartily ashamed."

Heath blinked, trying to collect himself and understand what it was his friend meant.

"Is there something wrong? What is it that troubles you?"

Lord Atherton shook his head.

"Is there something wrong?" he repeated under his breath, as though Heath was being deliberately obtuse. "You know very well that I am a foolish sort, do you not? Already, I have spoken of your desire to betroth yourself to a particular young lady, your desire to find a bride. I am sorry indeed for that."

Heath blinked. It had been some days since Lord Atherton had spoken so brashly and as yet, they had not had an opportunity to converse about what had taken place.

"You did stop yourself when I asked you to, did you not?" Heath spread his hands. "Though the damage is done, however, for I am now surrounded by young ladies who believe I might soon find one of them so delightful that I will seek to secure her as my bride. There are so many of them, I can barely distinguish one from the other." This was said with a rueful tilt of his lips, and Lord Atherton smiled briefly but did not look at Heath. Heaviness fell into Heath's stomach. "You have done something more?"

Lord Atherton closed his eyes.

"Unfortunately, yes." Lord Atherton dropped his head so low, his chin rested on his chest. "As you know, when I have imbibed a little too much, I struggle to speak with any consideration."

"What did you do?" Heath's heart began to slam hard in his chest as Lord Atherton ran one hand over his eyes. "And how does it affect me?"

"I may have suggested to Lady Gloucester that her daughter would be an excellent match for you, I believe I also stated that you had become acquainted with the young lady and were quite delighted with her."

Heath gritted his teeth, letting out a long breath that hissed out into the air between them.

"I do not even know who her daughter is."

"Yes, you do." Finally, Lord Atherton looked directly back at Heath. "She is Lady Margaret."

The moment that her name was said, Heath knew immediately who he was speaking of. Lady Margaret was an unexceptional young lady who seemed to think a great deal of herself. She spoke with a loud voice, declared her many fine attributes to anyone who would listen, and there-after went on to prove that she had *none* of the qualities which she believed herself to have. Her dancing was very poor, her conversation entirely lacking, unless they were talking about her, and her attempts at mirth were utterly uninspired.

"I would *never* consider Lady Margaret." Groaning, Heath looked back at his friend, utterly exasperated. "Whatever made you say such a thing?"

"I do not know." Lord Atherton let out a heavy sigh. "I

recall feeling entirely overwhelmed by Lady Gloucester's presence, for she was asking me questions about you. I was concerned, mayhap, that she would only be contented if I assured her that Lady Margaret had an opportunity to be your bride. Mayhap, to extricate myself from that situation, I then constructed this ridiculous lie. I am truly sorry for it."

"I can see that."

Lord Atherton's regret practically seeped out of him. With his drawn shoulders, his furrowed brow, and his scowl, Heath believed that the gentleman truly did regret what he had done. Unfortunately, this was now the second time that his friend had behaved foolishly, and it was becoming rather irritating.

Heath silently berated himself for saying anything to Lord Atherton in the first place. After all, his friend was known to have something of a loose tongue, was he not? Heath had foolishly believed that something this significant, something this severe, would be kept secret. What a misstep he had taken!

"I thought to come to tell you as soon as I could." Lord Atherton shook his head. "I know it makes very little difference given the fact that I behaved with such idiocy and lack of consideration, but it is the only apology I can give, and the only thing that I can do."

Letting out another long breath, Heath pinched the bridge of his nose.

"I shall have to make certain to avoid Lady Gloucester and her daughter at all costs."

"Then you may wish to begin at this very moment. As I came along the streets, having heard from your butler that you had gone into town, I am certain I saw the very lady in question walking here also."

Blinking rapidly, Heath looked around as though he

expected the young lady and her mother to be standing close by, waiting for him to turn and speak to them.

"I am afraid I shall have to take my leave, Atherton." Wishing he had taken his carriage rather than choosing to walk, Heath began to step away from his friend. "We shall talk about this matter later. At the moment, I think I shall return to my house."

"A wise idea."

Scurrying away, Heath kept his head low, no longer eager to be seen by anyone. His heart began to pound furiously, his steps quickening. Yes, he could hail a hackney, but that in itself might draw the attention of Lady Gloucester and her daughter, were they nearby. He was both relieved and irritated at Lord Atherton's behavior – irritated that he had said such a thing in the first place, but relieved that he had told him about it thereafter. Grimacing, he turned sharply into the corner of a slightly narrowed, darker lane, only for hands to grasp his arm and push him back against the wall as a low voice gritted out harsh words.

"So you decided to come to London for the Season."

Heath immediately tensed, pushing back against his opponent.

"Remove your hands from me!"

A low chuckle was his only answer as the man swung Heath around and put one hand around his shoulders, the pressure tight against his throat. Try as he might, Heath simply could not get free... and panic began to rise as his breathing became labored.

"But I know what you've done." The low voice seemed to growl as Heath fought to garner a look at the man's face, only to realize that he could not turn far enough to look over his shoulder since the man's grip was so tight. "Did you really think that you could just forget? That someone would not discover it, even though it happened some years ago?"

Something biting began to climb up Heath's chest, the fight going from him as he sagged back against the man, trying to get his breath. After a moment, the man laughed and shoved Heath away, so that he fell against the stone wall again, scratching his face against it. Staggering, Heath turned around, no strength in his limbs. The shadows were such that he could not make out the man's face, and he certainly did not recognize his voice. Whoever he was, he knew exactly what Heath had done, what he had spent the last five years trying to hide, and what he had been trying to forgive himself for.

"Do not touch me again." With a sudden burst of energy, Heath flung out one fist which the man only just avoided, swinging back into the shadows. "I know nothing of whatever you are speaking about."

"You would lie as well, my Lord?" The voice was low as the man moved forward again, his stance strong. "You would add to your guilt? You would suffer the consequences of yet more wrongdoing?"

"There is no need for any such thing." Speaking with more confidence than he felt, Heath took in a deep breath, resisting the urge to try to strike out again. It would do no good to do such a thing, even if that was his desire. The man could easily avoid him and he was still struggling to regain his breath. "Any matters of mine are precisely that: *mine*. I need no one else to attempt to point out any supposed guilt, nor do I appreciate being set upon in such a manner." Making certain not to admit to anything, he took a deep breath and then lifted both hands, curling them into fists. Now he had regained himself a little, Heath was a good deal more confident.

"You will need to remove yourself from my presence immediately."

Fighting would do nothing other than cause them both some injuries, but Heath was not about to allow this fellow to continue in such a manner. The silent threat was there, and after some moments the man opposite him eventually stepped back, holding up both hands. Taking a breath, Heath lifted his chin and went to walk straight past him, resisting the urge to grab out at him again, only for the fellow to whirl around and grasp his shoulder. His fingers dug into Heath, his voice whispering into his ear, sending shudders running over his skin.

"Such behavior cannot go without punishment, my Lord." A quiet malevolent chuckle whispered through the air. "Have no doubt, consequences will come to you soon enough. I am to make sure of it."

Before Heath could respond, the man had melted into the gloom of the street. Thoughts and fears immediately began to fill Heath's head and, although he forced his steps back out towards the main street, he could not help but feel a quickening of doubt within his soul. How was it the man knew what he had done? He had spent the last few years trying to ignore his guilt, trying to push it away, trying to pretend that he had done nothing wrong, and that it was for everyone's good that he had behaved as he did. Now, however, it seemed that someone had learned of what he had done. Someone who had kept it to themselves thus far, and perhaps intended to use it against him – though what their motivation was, he could not tell. Had they been sent by his brother? Had his brother learned the truth? Surely it could not be.

But if it is so, there is nothing I can do other than to accept my fate.

"Perhaps this is what I deserve."

Muttering to himself, he took off his hat and, with his handkerchief, wiped at the sweat beading on his forehead. He did not know where he was going, he was walking rather blindly, as though his past sins might chase after him, even now. Was he to be punished for the choice he had made? And just when would those consequences come – and by whose hand?

"Oh Lord Landon, Lord Landon!"

Heath blinked rapidly, soon realizing that the voice calling him was none other than that of Lady Gloucester, who approached, her daughter following her closely. Both women had bright eyes and broad smiles, and yet Heath could not shake off the darkness which now clung to him, wrapping around him like a coat he was forced to wear.

"Good afternoon, Lady Gloucester, Lady Margaret." He bowed sharply, having no interest in speaking with them at length about anything. "I confess I must take my leave. An urgent matter has called me back to my house."

"As long as it does not call you back to your estate... at least, not without a wife!" Lady Gloucester practically beamed at him. "It is understandable for a gentleman to be so very busy. Tell me, do you plan to attend the soiree this evening? You have been invited to Lord Ludford's little gathering, I am sure. He does tell me that there is to be some excellent entertainment."

Trying desperately to recall whether or not he had been invited to any such thing, Heath ended up clearing his throat.

"I am not certain of my plans for this evening." This was the only thing he could say, the only answer he could provide given how clouded his mind was, but it did not seem to satisfy Lady Gloucester, nor her daughter, and they both frowned. Heath shrugged his shoulders. "If I am still able to attend, then of course, I shall."

"I should be very glad if you would do so."

Lady Margaret's expression immediately began to light up, as she sent him a warm smile.

"And if you should like to sit with my daughter for the entertainment, then –"

"I am afraid that I cannot give any guarantee to that." Breaking into Lady Gloucester's speech rather sharply, Heath dismissed her surprised expression. "And I should also state that I am aware that there are some rumors going around London about me and my present situation." He was speaking a little more brusquely now, being a good deal more open than he ought, but he was growing tired of ladies pressing towards him when they did not even know him. Would he be ever able to tell any of them what it was he had done? Would he trust any of them with his guilt, now that it had been brought back so sharply into focus? If he was to ever tell a young lady of his acquaintance what he had done, then would she turn her back on him? Would she, even as his bride, reject him? However, was he to find himself in a happy situation if he could not be honest with his own wife, whoever she might be? "I pray you to forgive me for speaking so plainly, Lady Gloucester, but I have no desire for a bride at present. I am afraid that Lord Atherton decided to speak so simply to provoke me." He managed to force his lips into a wry smile. "I should not want to disappoint any young lady and thus thought it best to inform you that I simply intend to enjoy the London Season by conversing, eating and drinking, dancing, and, of course, making some new acquaintances. I have no intention of taking anyone as a bride, as yet, however."

Heath watched the light fade from Lady Gloucester's

eyes. She was clearly disappointed, her jaw now tight, her brow furrowing. Her daughter also began to sink into herself, her shoulders dropping low, her hands clasping tightly in front of her, and her gaze immediately began to drift away. To Heath's mind, this proved that the only reason they were interested in his company was because of his supposed desire for matrimony. Once news spread around London, no doubt he would find himself with considerably fewer young ladies eager for his attention.

"I see." Lady Gloucester managed a smile, although it faded soon after. "I do not think it is particularly amusing for Lord Atherton to do so. Such things are not to be taken lightly."

"I quite agree."

Heath inclined his head, glancing at Lady Margaret and seeing how quickly she had moved away from him. Her body was shifted to one side, her eyes moving around the streets as though she might want to find someone else to speak with almost at once. He was to be a gentleman quickly forgotten, simply because he had made it clear that matrimony was no longer his priority.

His heart dropped low.

I could never invite a young lady into this situation. Not now. Not when there may be consequences to face.

Swallowing hard, he quickly bid farewell to Lady Gloucester and her daughter. The situation had changed now. It was much too difficult for him to even *consider* bringing a bride into his life. Whoever had discovered what he had done, he would have to face that first and deal with whatever recompense they wanted, before he could allow himself such happiness as a wife. Even if the matter was brought to a conclusion, would he ever be strong enough to tell his wife the truth about what he had done, so long ago?

Would he risk her disdain? Her dislike, her upset, her confusion? Would he do so, knowing that she would think less of him? Groaning, Heath turned his steps towards home. He planned to walk inside that sanctuary, close the door, and remain there for some time. Perhaps then this new, painful darkness would retreat a little. Or mayhap, it was coming to find him regardless, creeping in around the edges, sending shadows through his life until he was forced to face the penalty he had been avoiding for so long.

CHAPTER FOUR

"I'm afraid I will have to take my leave."

Bridget caught her breath in surprise. Lord Landon had only been sitting for a few minutes and now was already intending to take his leave. She caught her mother and sister sharing a glance and immediately flushed with mortification. She had been waiting in eager expectation for Lord Landon's visit but had done her level best not to appear overly delighted about it, telling her mother of it quite calmly, as though it were to be expected that a gentleman would come to call upon her. Inwardly, however, she had exulted in the fact that a handsome, amiable, eligible gentleman - one who was apparently looking for a bride, according to rumor – desired to come to call on her. Now, however, it seemed that his visit was going to be nothing more than a mortification rather than a joy. He was not to stay. He was not about to enjoy any time with her. Instead, he was simply going to sit for a few minutes, say very little, and thereafter, take his leave.

"But we have not even poured the tea, Lord Landon." Still highly embarrassed, Bridget took a deep breath, forcing a smile to her lips that she did not feel. "Surely you will stay for a few minutes longer?"

Lord Landon looked at her, his eyes heavy with a shadow she had not seen before.

"I am afraid I cannot."

Hot tears immediately began to spring into Bridget's eyes, but she refused to let them fall. The last thing she required at present was to lose her composure in front of her mother and her sister.

"But of course."

There was the tiniest wobble to her voice, the smallest indication that she was upset, and, instantly, Lord Landon looked directly at her, his eyebrows lifting. Then he closed his eyes for a moment, letting out a long breath as though he regretted what he had said.

"It is most disappointing that I have to make my visit so short." He spoke more firmly now, his tone a little darker. "I can assure you, this was not my intention. I thought to take tea with you and stay for a prolonged length of time." As Bridget blinked away her tears, Lord Landon turned his attention directly to Bridget's mother. "I must apologize for departing so quickly, Lady Culpepper. Unfortunately, a matter has come to my hand, and must be dealt with every swiftness."

In response, Lady Culpepper waved one hand in Bridget's direction.

"Then you need not have called!" She trilled a laugh, which seemed entirely out of place given the evident seriousness of the conversation. "Bridget would not have minded. It is not as though she has any expectations. I am certain that she would have been more than happy to wait for your visit at another time."

Bridget's stomach swirled, her face burning as her mother so quickly and easily dismissed her.

"Ah, but I would never do such a thing to Miss Wynch." Lord Landon turned and threw Bridget a brief smile though his brows remained knotted. "I should not have liked to rearrange for another time, as I was looking forward to my visit. Even though this visit has been short, I am very glad to have seen you for a short while, Miss Wynch." Again, his smile was offered in her direction but still, his eyes remained dark and heavy. "I am very sorry, Miss Wynch, to be so brief. Mayhap you would allow me to call upon you again very soon?"

The tears which had been threatening now left, for there was no requirement for them any longer, not when Lord Landon had made himself so very obvious in front of both her mother and her sister. She smiled at him, gratitude overwhelming her.

"I should like that very much. At your earliest convenience, of course."

Lord Landon rose to his feet and the three ladies followed suit. He bowed first to Lady Culpepper, nodded to her sister, and then, much to Bridget's surprise, drew near to her.

"I am sorry."

With a quick move, he reached for her hand, and she gave it for him to bow over, though his lips did not touch her skin. His hot breath, however, ran across her skin, and Bridget caught her breath. Her affections were already engaged with this gentleman, she realized with a gentle horror, as those affections wrapped their tendrils around her already fragile heart. His eyes lifted to hers as he rose, and Bridget shivered from the top of her head to the tips of her toes.

"Please, do not apologize. I quite understand." Again, there was a slight quaver to her voice - a sound that she hated, for it gave so much of herself away. "Do not have any great concern on my part. I will look forward to your next visit whenever it shall be."

In saying such a thing, she did allow him the opportunity to tell her when he might stop by next, whether it be within the next sennight or even the next fortnight, but his response did not come. He did not promise her anything but, instead, merely nodded, smiled briefly, and then stepped away.

The instant he removed himself from the room, a slight chill came over Bridget's skin. Had the room suddenly dropped in temperature? With a light shudder, she sat back down, her thoughts weighted and heavy.

"Well." Lady Culpepper's voice was a little soft. "It seems as though Lord Landon truly *was* disappointed at having to end his visit so quickly." Was it disbelief that added to the quietness to her tone? "I do wonder about why he had to step away so hastily. Gentlemen often call for a short time, but not as short as that."

Bridget said nothing, trying to smile, and yet feeling the heavy weight of Lord Landon's hasty absence. She was relieved, however, that her mother had not said anything to add to her confusion, and that Sophia had also said very little. She did not want her sister's mockery to add to her already pained heart.

"Lord Landon is an exceptionally eligible gentleman, is he not, Mama?"

Her mother considered Sophia's remark, tilting her head one way and then the other.

"Yes, which is why, I confess, I would be surprised if he

was truly considering Bridget. It does seem as though his interest is a little piqued, however."

Bridget said nothing, only closing her eyes and tightening one hand into a fist. It was as though she were entirely absent from the room!

"Alas, I believe you are mistaken, Mama."

Bridget's eyes flew open as Sophia sat quietly in her chair, her gaze fixed on their mother.

"Whatever do you mean Sophia?" Lady Culpepper waved a hand. "It is well known amongst society that Lord Landon has declared himself eager to wed. As I have said, I would be a little astonished if he were truly interested in Bridget, but such things have happened before."

It was as though her mother did not think her words would cause Bridget any pain, given how lightly she spoke to them. Bridget, however, was forced to swallow down the anger which began to bubble up within her at how quickly, and how easily, her mother dismissed her – and without any real reason for doing so, other than the fact that she did not bear the same beauty as her sister.

Sophia turned her head and caught Bridget's gaze, a cool, delicate smile on her lips that did not speak of any warmth or affection.

"It is only to say, Mama, that I have heard say that Lord Landon has no intention of seeking a bride whatsoever!"

Her smile grew as Bridget's spirits were instantly flattened.

"How do you know such a thing?" Lady Culpepper's tone was now one of annoyance. "I have heard very differently from my acquaintances."

"I have heard it from Lady Margaret." Sophia's voice was soft, as though she were sympathetic about what this might mean for Bridget, although her lingering smile stated that she felt no such thing. "You know how gentlemen can be. A little liquor can cause a great deal of foolishness, it seems."

Lady Culpepper took in a deep breath, throwing up her hands before letting them fall to her lap.

"Well, that is it then."

"At least it is plain for you to see, Bridget. Lord Landon is simply an amiable fellow who has taken a little pity on you. He has seen that you are inclined to hang about the shadows of a room, and wishes to show a little kindness, that is all." Sophia sighed and shrugged as Bridget's stomach twisted hard. "Shall I ring the bell for a fresh tea tray, Mama?"

Lady Culpepper nodded.

"Shall you join us, Bridget, since you did not manage to drink anything with Lord Landon?"

Everything within Bridget encouraged her to remain seated, to put on a demeanor of strength, but one glimpse at her sister's delicate features still encased in that cold smile told Bridget that she could not do so.

"Thank you, Mama, but I think I shall excuse myself for a short while."

Her mother merely nodded and then began to converse with Sophia about what gown she would be wearing to tomorrow evening's ball. Bridget hurried to the door to make her escape, her heart crying out so painfully that tears pressed themselves to her eyes. Pulling out her handker-chief, she dabbed at her cheeks as she scurried up to her bedchamber where she might give in to her sadness in solitude.

~

"You look a little sad." Miss Millington slipped one arm through Bridget's as they walked together. "In fact, you have appeared quite sorrowful these last two days."

Bridget let out a small breath.

"I am sure that you have heard the news about Lord Landon."

Miss Millington frowned.

"No, I have not."

The words brought pain to Bridget's heart as she spoke them.

"It seems as though he is not intending to wed after all."

"But the entirety of the *ton* believes he is to do so." Miss Millington's surprise echoed through her voice. "Do you mean to say that now he has decided against the idea? He will leave a good many disappointed young ladies."

"Of whom I am one." Bridget did not mind mentioning such a thing aloud, for their friendship was such that she was able to be honest with her friend without being over-whelmed. "You will think me foolish for letting my heart be so affected by the gentleman so quickly, but he is the first fellow who has ever shown any sort of interest. When he came to call some two days ago, I was filled with delight, hope, and expectation. But a few minutes was all the time he could give me. He said he wished to call again soon, but gave me no indication as to when it would be."

She shook her head.

There was a short silence. Bridget did not mind it for, in the quiet moments, she was able to grasp hold of her own emotions and bring them back under control. She could not lose her composure in the middle of Hyde Park!

"I am sorry to hear that you have been disappointed by him – but certainly, I do not think you foolish."

"He has not disappointed me in any way. He has no

responsibility towards me, has made no promise to be broken." Taking in a somewhat shaky breath, Bridget let it out again slowly before she continued. "I should not have allowed my heart to be affected by him, but he had such a kind and generous character, I could not help but find myself drawn to him... only to realize now that he does not have any particular feelings for me."

"You cannot know that for certain." Miss Millington gave her a small smile. "Mayhap you should use 'The London Ledger' to make certain of it."

Bridget offered her friend a wry look.

"I do not think there is any purpose behind doing so. I was taken in by his charm and allowed myself to dream of his consideration. I have no one to blame in that but myself."

"I would encourage you to do so nonetheless." Miss Millington offered her another encouragement, squeezing her hand. "After all, he did say that he wished to call upon you again?"

Sighing, Bridget nodded.

"Though I have no expectation of him doing so. As I have said, I suspect that he spoke as such, simply to do so in front of my mother and sister. I believe he said such things only to make certain that I should not be teased by my sister, such was the generosity of his thinking... which does make him appear to be all the more kind-hearted. I cannot help but think well of him."

"I think you should certainly place something in 'The London Ledger'." From over her shoulder came a clear, confident voice. Turning her head, she saw Lady Yardley smiling at her. Hurrying forward, she came to join them both. "You will have to forgive me for eavesdropping. I was, in fact, coming to speak with you about Lord Landon when

I heard Miss Millington do the very same. Her suggestion is a wise one. The gentleman may be a little confused over what he desires and, to find out for certain, you might use 'The London Ledger'."

The urge to say yes grew swiftly and it was on the tip of Bridget's tongue to say that yes, she would do so, only for her to hold herself back.

"I do not know what the consequences would be if I were to do so." She shook her head. "Nor do I wish to upset him. If I am to be honest, I find it more and more difficult to believe that Lord Landon could be truly interested in me."

"But we do not." Lady Yardley's voice softened. "You are just as eligible, just as beautiful, and just as amiable as many of the young ladies here this summer – if not more so."

"Which means it is quite proper for a gentleman such as Lord Landon to be interested in you." Miss Millington pressed her arm a little. "To our eyes, he *has* shown you some particular interest."

Surprised, and a little embarrassed, Bridget considered their words, but her heart continued to sink. She dropped her head, her sigh slowly escaping her.

"You do not believe it." Lady Yardley shook her head, touching Bridget's arm lightly as she did so. "My dear young lady, I can assure you that you have so much beauty about you, it will be a fortunate gentleman who takes you as his bride."

"You will not always have to be in the shadow of your sister." Miss Millington spoke firmly, sending small spirals of pain into Bridget's heart. "I am aware of how much your mother supports her, and how little she turns to you, but I can promise you that everything Lady Yardley has said is true. I beg of you not to give up on Lord Landon, and on what your heart feels for him." Miss Millington leaned towards her a little more, their steps slower now. "That is what we each seek, is it not? We seek a love match, and if your heart is beginning to involve itself with this gentleman, then do not force yourself to forget him. Such feelings do not often arise, so I have been told, but when they do, they should be held with great carefulness."

Bridget took a deep breath. Her friend was speaking the truth, she knew, but there was so much that she struggled to accept. Admitting that her heart felt something significant for Lord Landon was not a difficulty in itself, but the realization that her feelings might not be returned was bringing her more pain than she had anticipated.

"Very well." She looked to Lady Yardley. "I do not know what exactly I should ask to be placed into 'The London Ledger', however. I know that all of society will read it, but I do not want to do anything to injure Lord Landon."

"I will simply state what has been said." Lady Yardley nodded slowly, her eyes drifting away from Bridget, as she was clearly thinking through what would be required. "As you know, I am the one who both writes and permits various other writings to be placed within the Ledger. I have always been careful to print either what is true, or to state that the rumors and whispers which are spoken of are precisely that. Therefore, I will do much the same with Lord Landon." She shrugged both shoulders. "No doubt the gentleman will clarify his position very soon thereafter, and there will be no doubt as to where you stand with him." Bridget nodded slowly, taking a breath and then releasing it again. She was rather unsettled at the thought of placing such a thing in 'The London Ledger', a little concerned about what would come thereafter, but then, she considered, at the very least, she would know precisely what Lord Landon sought for himself. "I will not do this unless you are entirely contented." Lady Yardley's soft tones broke through Bridget's thoughts. "You must decide what you want. I will not force you in any direction."

Setting her shoulders, Bridget lifted her chin.

"Miss Millington is quite correct. I *do* find myself eager to keep hold of my feelings as regards Lord Landon, even if my fears try to push me away from him. If there is even the smallest hope, then I should like to know of it."

It was a little discomforting to speak so honestly, but both Miss Millington and Lady Yardley smiled their agreement, clearly delighted that she had come to such a conclusion.

"I shall write it this very afternoon." Lady Yardley spoke briskly. "It will go to be printed this evening, for distribution tomorrow. I have no doubt, Miss Wynch, that we will soon discover exactly what it is which Lord Landon desires for himself this London Season, and then you will know precisely where it is you stand."

"IT IS READY."

Bridget took a deep breath. Lady Yardley had asked her to call so that they might make sure that the wording to be placed within 'The London Ledger' was precisely as Bridget wanted. Now it was completed, ready for publication. Her gaze rested on the papers in Lady Yardley's hands.

"This will all be ready for tomorrow?"

"If not, then the day afterward." Lady Yardley came towards her, setting the papers down on the table as she went. "I will only publish this if you are quite certain that it is what you desire. Again, I ask you so that I do not put you under any pressure to do as *I* think is right."

Bridget shook her head, appreciating Lady Yardley's concern.

"I am quite contented. What you have written is very carefully worded and yet, at the same time, it will help us to find out the truth about Lord Landon's current intentions for the Season."

The older lady held Bridget's gaze for some moments before eventually stepping away, ready to pick up the papers again.

"Then I shall take this to the publishers myself. I may be a little tardy this evening, however. There is much I need to do before this evening's soiree, but I have every intention of taking the Ledger to the publishers before the afternoon is out!"

"Could I not take it for you?" Gesturing to the clock, Bridget smiled a little ruefully. "My mother has very little idea of where I am at present, and certainly will not care until the moment we are to leave for the soiree this evening – the same one you will be attending. I had thought to go to the orphanage for a short while before I returned home, and I would be glad to take the Ledger to the publishers for you on my way."

Lady Yardley considered for a moment, her head tilting a little.

"That is very kind of you. Only if it would not be too much trouble."

"It would be no trouble at all. I should be very pleased to take it."

Lady Yardley beamed at her.

"Thank you. You have a kind heart, Miss Wynch. Might I ask how often you go to the orphanage?"

Bridget shrugged.

"It varies, depending on what time I have available. This afternoon, however, I have nothing to encroach on my time, save to make certain that I am ready for the soiree. As you know, my mother and father will not even question me about where I have been, and there is some advantage in that."

"I suppose there is some advantage." Lady Yardley shook her head, her smile sad as she handed the papers that would become the next edition of 'The London Ledger' to Bridget. "Although I imagine it must be a little lonely."

Something lurched in Bridget's chest.

"It can be," she admitted as Lady Yardley nodded. "But I am all the more grateful for my friends... and for you also."

Lady Yardley took her hand for a moment and pressed it.

"One day a gentleman will realize just how extraordinary a creature you are," she told Bridget, who immediately felt tears begin to burn in the edges of her eyes. "Do not stand in the shadows any longer, my dear. Stand with your friends, stand with me if you wish, but do not hide any longer. You are worth far more than you have been led to believe, and I am certain that, one day soon, a gentleman of worth will see that, and will make you the happiest creature that has ever been."

STEPPING OUT OF THE CARRIAGE, Bridget looked around. She had been expecting a dark, and perhaps somewhat dingy, street in a slightly less reputable area of town, but all in all, it appeared to be quite respectable. A few shops stood side by side, their banners declaring what they sold. The publishers were easy enough to see and thus, Bridget began to make her way towards the door, waving away the concern of her coachman and footman.

"I shall only be a few minutes."

Making her way along the street, Bridget was suddenly caught by a strong arm. Something furious seemed to explode around her and she staggered forward, only to be hauled back. Before she could realize what was happening, she had been shoved back hard against the wall of a shop, her bonnet twisted uncomfortably, her head aching from where it had slammed against the brick, her knuckles scraping on the rough stone as she fought to catch herself. Fighting for breath, trying to understand what had happened, she blinked furiously, her body burning with a fierce strength that pushed her to her feet.

Her footman ran towards her, his voice seeming to sound very far away, even though he was looking directly into her face. "Miss Wynch! Are you all right?"

"I am." One hand ran over her eyes as the footman helped her to stand. "The papers?"

The footman shook his head as Bridget managed to focus on him.

"That young man had no thought as to where he was going." Tutting lightly, he clicked his tongue, his hand still around Bridget's arm. "I should take you back to the carriage."

Bridget took a deep breath. She was not about to collapse to the ground or any such thing and, despite her legs trembling a little still, she gestured to the fallen papers as they lay on the ground at her feet.

"Please fetch my papers. I must get them to the publisher."

The footman looked at her for a moment, perhaps a

little uncertain as to whether or not he could release her arm, only to do so with great caution. Then, keeping one eye on her, he went to pick up the various pieces of paper which were scattered about. Deeply concerned over what had happened, Bridget made to reach for one also, only for her vision to begin to blur. Putting one hand to her head, she let out a slow breath and the footman was once more at her side.

"I think you should go to the carriage, my lady." His concern shone in his eyes. "I can take these papers to the publishers for you. You should sit and rest and we will take you back to the house rather than going to the orphanage."

Bridget shook her head and then immediately regretted doing so.

"I shall be quite well." Swallowing, she tried to smile as the footman's frown only grew. "I shall allow you to take those papers to the publishers, but thereafter we will make our way to the orphanage as we had planned."

The footman's jaw tightened, but he said nothing. Leading her back to the carriage, he ensured that she was safely inside before he turned back to the publishing house. Letting out a slow breath, Bridget leaned her head back against the squabs gingerly, wincing as pain surfaced once more. That had been most unfortunate. She could only hope that Lady Yardley understood, and would not be in any way concerned over what had taken place. The last thing Bridget wanted was to upset the lady, not when she had done so much for her.

"It was only an accident."

Murmuring to herself, Bridget kept her eyes tight shut as the footman climbed back up to his seat beside the coachman. Reaching up, she rapped on the roof. and after a moment, the horses began to move forward.

Bridget dropped her shoulders and closed her eyes again. Despite the trouble, she had done as she had offered and delivered the papers to the publishing house – albeit with the help of her footman. Now all she could do was wait and see just how Lord Landon responded to his name being in print. Very soon, she would discover whether or not he was worth waiting for.

CHAPTER FIVE

"*I* must do something."

Muttering to himself, Heath paced up and down the room, one hand threading through his hair over and over again. He was struggling with his conscience. Ever since that fellow had whispered the threat of consequences into his ear, he had become anxious, worrying about what would happen and battling the fresh sense of guilt which now captured him. Nothing had come of it as yet, but he was still concerned that something would be told to the *ton,* and he would then be left to mingle amongst a society that considered him both unworthy and unwelcome.

And I cannot continue my acquaintance with Miss Wynch, no matter how much I might wish it.

Sighing, Heath pinched the bridge of his nose, screwing his eyes up tightly. He had been deeply frustrated by realizing that he had to step away from her, but with these threats coming, he *had* to protect her. If the truth came out, and they were rather closely acquainted, then he would not be able to protect her reputation from being tainted by his past sins. To step away was the only thing he could do, for certain, he could not prevent her from hearing terrible things of him - things he was ashamed of, things he feared, and things he had believed were well hidden but which now appeared to be inescapable.

Perhaps there is a way that I can make up for my sin?

Rubbing one hand over his chin, Heath made his way to the window to look out upon the London streets. Perhaps if he were seen doing good works, then the threats would fade away. It was a very faint hope – most likely a foolish one – but might it make a difference?

It would soothe my tortured conscience.

Taking a deep breath, Heath closed his eyes. When he resided at his estate, there were always many endeavors he put his mind and his coin to, including caring for those who did not have a great deal. He had done so for the last few years, finding himself desirous to do it – but mayhap it had also come as a way to push away some of his shame over what he had done.

Could he not do the same here? Surely there would be many more who required his aid here in London! Setting his shoulders, Heath nodded to himself as he turned on his heel and went to pull the bell. This was something he could focus his time on, at least. With this, he might find forgiveness, and perhaps find a way of removing some of the heavy weight which had settled upon his soul.

"Yes, my Lord?"

"I need to know the areas of London which are the most impoverished."

The butler, who normally remained quite impassive, allowed a flicker to come into his eyes.

"My Lord?"

"I wish to be involved in some charitable works." Explaining quickly, Heath shrugged both shoulders as though the matter was not of significance. "I have done so at my estate and wish to do the same here. I am sure you can understand."

"But of course." The butler cleared his throat lightly, then placed both hands behind his back, his shoulders pulled back a little. "How very gracious of you, my Lord. Allow me to consider for a moment."

Heath said nothing, although inwardly rolling his eyes. The butler would, of course, give as many compliments as he could, simply because Heath was his master and he the servant.

"There are many orphanages, my Lord, and a good many poorhouses also. I am certain that they would always be glad of your coin."

Heath nodded slowly, considering.

"I think I should like to visit such a place before I commit my efforts." He remarked as the butler's eyes widened, clearly unable to keep his surprise at bay this time. "I think I shall visit an orphanage. I should like to see what it is that they do, and where any donation of mine would go. Might you suggest one?"

The butler blinked rapidly, then allowed his hands to drop to his sides.

"I have heard that the Dove Street Orphanage is one of the largest on this side of London," he answered, as Heath began to nod his agreement. "I am certain that they would always be glad of some charity, although, might I say, my Lord that, if you do not wish to attend in person, I am sure that –"

"No, I am quite able to attend in person. I wish to do so." Clearing his throat, he gestured to the butler. "In fact, make the carriage ready. I should like to go this very afternoon."

The butler hesitated for only a fraction of a second before he turned to do Heath's bidding. A sense of contentment slowly began to seep into Heath's soul as the servant hurried away. This, perhaps, was what was required for his guilt to begin to diminish. He might also hope that the threat of dire consequences which had been whispered into his ear would not come to pass if he was seen to be giving to charitable causes and the like. Taking a deep breath, Heath made his way to the door, hurrying down the staircase so that he might fetch his hat and his gloves. There was no time to lose. The visit to the orphanage was now of great importance to him and he did not want to delay even for a moment.

WALKING into the orphanage was not something Heath had prepared himself for. The moment he set foot inside, he realized how hasty he had been in his decision to come here. A great cloud of shame washed over him, turning his face hot as he considered his motivations for attending. Of course, those who worked here immediately began to express their delight at his willingness to even *look* at the children they cared for here, thanking him for his offer of some financial assistance, and yet Heath's guilt only grew. The main reason he had come here was in an attempt to ease his conscience - a conscience he had been attempting to ignore for the last few years.

It was a wrong, and very selfish, motivation and Heath admitted that to himself, his head dropping forward.

"As you may know, we are the largest orphanage on this side of London." Mrs. Martin – a rather large, burly sort of woman - walked alongside him, gesturing to the children as she went. "We have new children arriving every day." Much to Heath's surprise, the children were not running around, behaving in an unruly manner, and unengaged, but rather acted with a calmness of spirit and clear adherence to the rules which had been set out for them. Then again, he considered that with a severe woman like Mrs. Martin running the orphanage, even he would fear stepping out of line. "The orphanage is at present undergoing some repairs, and we have to constantly seek out more money to make sure that we are providing the best possible care for these poor orphaned souls."

Heath lifted an eyebrow but said nothing, silently thinking that Mrs. Martin was doing what she could to pull at his heartstrings by speaking in such plain terms, but she need not do so. Guilt abounded within him already, guilt over the fact that he had come here in an attempt to quieten his shame, without having any real consideration for those present here. But now he was here, looking about him, now he was taking in the situation, seeing the children, and realizing how much need there was, his guilt continued to overwhelm him. He had so much, and they had so little, but was it truly enough just to throw some coin in the direction of Mrs. Martin and hope that it would be enough to assuage his guilt? Any gentleman or lady could do such a thing. They could give money without so much as a thought, telling themselves they were doing something good, something which would bring ease or comfort to those who needed it while, at the same time, alleviating their own conscience. No doubt many of them would be more than a little surprised to see him here – but ought he not to be giving a little of himself to those who had so little?

Heath was pulled from his thoughts by a sudden

glimpse of a young lady – a young lady who he was certain he recognized.

"Good gracious!"

It took him a moment to catch himself and then Mrs. Martin was at his elbow, gesturing in the same direction as Heath was looking.

"Yes, that is a young lady by the name of Miss Wynch." The gentle smile on Mrs. Martin's face told Heath everything he needed to know about the situation, and just how pleased Mrs. Martin was with Miss Wynch's presence. "As you can see, she gives her time to come and care for the girls here. She makes sure that their hair is clean, brushed, and braided. They appreciate her a great deal." She tilted her head, looking at him. "You may think such a thing to not be very important, but I can promise you, her gentle conversation, quiet manner, and obvious care for these young girls does a great deal for them – and for all of us."

Heath nodded, his gaze still on the young lady as his heart began to quicken from its steady beat. As yet, Miss Wynch had not noticed him, for she was standing at an angle, brushing a young girl's hair with long, gentle strokes. He took in her profile, seeing how she smiled and hearing the young girl laugh in return. His heart lurched. He had never expected to see such beauty as Miss Wynch standing here, doing something so simple as brushing hair, as though this was precisely where she wanted to be. How much he admired her for giving up her time in such a way!

"Would you like to go and speak with her?"

Starting visibly at Mrs. Martin's voice, Heath shook his head.

"No. No, I should not like to interrupt her." It was an excuse, of course, for he could not fully explain his reluctance. But something about seeing her here, something that came with the awareness of how much she was giving, compared to how much he was attempting to take for himself, made him less than eager to go to her. Quite the opposite, he wanted to shrink away. "She does look very busy, and I am sure it would not be particularly enjoyable for those girls to have her taken away from them."

Mrs. Martin smiled as though he were somehow the very best of gentlemen for thinking so kindly of the girls within the orphanage.

"Of course. Right this way."

With relief, Heath followed Mrs. Martin, but not before casting one more glance towards Miss Wynch. With his situation currently as difficult as it appeared, his thoughts about courting the young lady now fled from him. How could he, when there was such a threat hanging over his head, when his guilt had come to seek him out again? How could he even go about telling Miss Wynch what had taken place?

The shame of it would be far too much to bear. No, he resolved silently. walking all the more swiftly away from her, no, he could not tell Miss Wynch - or anyone else within society - of what he had done. Yes, it was some time ago, but that did not mean that his sin did not linger, the weight of it now brought back to full life by the threat of heavy consequences which had come to settle upon his shoulders.

It was not as though he could go back on what he had done, not as though he could change it in some way to make it more acceptable. Rather, he was left to linger upon the choice he had made and what had followed since then. Even though he had told himself repeatedly that his trans-gression had been in the best interests of not only his family line but also, at the time, his father, he had never been able to fully cover over the guilt his actions had brought with them.

And now, someone was threatening him. Someone who had somehow discovered his wrongdoing and now intended to use his guilt against him.

But if I confess, then the guilt might fade.

That option came with the risk of being rejected. He could be pushed away by society, scorned, rejected, and his reputation irredeemably scarred. People would speak of him in harsh whispers. He would garner nothing but angry looks and horrified expressions. They would murmur about him until the day he died - and any child he bore might have to endure the same. No, the threat was much too great, the suffering too immense to even contemplate.

The only thing left for him to do was wait.

CHAPTER SIX

"*W*ell?"

Bridget licked her lips.

"He is not here as yet."

Lady Almeria looked around the room.

"I am sure that he will arrive soon. I am certain the gentleman will wish to clarify his position just as soon as he reads 'The London Ledger'."

Given the way that Bridget's hands curled into fists, she was quite certain that she did *not* have the calm outward expression she had intended. She had barely slept the previous evening, afraid now that she might have made the wrong choice in agreeing to this article being placed within the Ledger.

"What if, in doing as I have done, I have chased the gentleman away from London? What if he leaves society and returns to his estate?"

Lady Almeria smiled softly.

"A highly unlikely scenario. Do not become over-wrought, he will not do so – and even if he should, then, as much as it pains me to say it, you will be in a better position, my dear friend, because you will know whether or not there is any worth in offering him your heart." Her voice dropped to a quieter tone. "I have every hope he will prove himself worthy, however." Bridget swallowed hard and tried to take some of her friend's certainty for herself. Her connection to Lord Landon was not of any great strength as yet but there certainly was something between them, something she very much wished to explore and to deepen if she could – but only if he was as eager as she. "You need not look so worried." Lady Almeria smiled and wrapped one arm around Bridget's shoulders. "You know that nothing untoward has been discovered about his character. He is not a gentleman known to be either a rogue or a scoundrel. He does not even have any particular interest in gambling either, or so it seems!"

Nodding, Bridget kept her counsel. Lady Yardley had made one or two discrete inquiries, but they had returned nothing of concern about Lord Landon's character. This in itself was a good thing, but it did not explain his sudden absence from her company. Hopefully what had been placed in 'The London Ledger' would clarify for her exactly what his position was on matrimony and, in turn, would bring her some peace of mind.

"Have you had anything to eat?" Miss Millington came to join them, gesturing to the tables spread with many delicacies. Seeing Bridget shake her head, she let out a small sigh. "It is an afternoon tea, my dear friend. You should eat something."

Bridget shook her head again.

"I do not think I could. I am so very nervous about 'The London Ledger'. Did you say Lady Yardley would bring one here this afternoon?"

"She intends to, certainly." Miss Millington smiled, only

for her eyes to brighten as she gestured across the room. "Look, there she is. She must have only just arrived."

Bridget was about to smile in greeting, only to note the way that Lady Yardley grasped 'The London Ledger' in her hand. Her knuckles were white, there was no smile on her face of welcome, and rather than looking in any way glad to see them, she appeared somewhat displeased. Her eyes were fixed on Bridget, and she came directly towards them with short, hurried steps.

"Miss Wynch." Lady Yardley stopped in front of her, taking a moment before she continued as though fighting to keep control of herself. "I must ask you precisely what happened yesterday."

From the slight narrowing of Lady Yardley eyes, Bridget suddenly began to fear that she had done something wrong.

"I do not understand." Her breath began to come a little more quickly. "Yesterday?"

"With the papers, Miss Wynch." Lady Yardley spoke quickly, waving 'The London Ledger' about with one hand. "Did you take it to the publishers as I requested?"

She nodded quickly.

"Yes, I did."

Lady Yardley's gaze grew all the more intense.

"And did you replace any of these pages?"

Blinking in surprise, Bridget lifted her chin, confidence flooding her.

"I certainly did not."

For some moments, there was nothing but silence as Lady Yardley searched Bridget's face while her heart continued to pound furiously. She had, for some reason, garnered Lady Yardley's ire. She could not understand it, could not comprehend why there was such upset, and it was only when Lady Yardley closed her eyes and let out a heavy sigh that Bridget finally found herself able to breathe again.

"Is something wrong?" Miss Millington, clearly aware of the tension, glanced from Lady Yardley to Bridget and back again. "Has something happened with the Ledger?"

Lady Yardley closed her eyes, letting out a slow breath.

"Something *has* happened. I do not know how or why. Mayhap I should speak to the publishers, but my first thought was...."

Her gaze went to Bridget and then away again.

Bridget swallowed hard.

"Your first thought was that I had done something to change part of the Ledger," she finished on Lady Yardley's behalf. "Why would you think such a thing?"

Her hands began to curl into tight fists, her heart caught with a flash of anger.

"Because of what has been written about Lord Landon." Her arms spread wide for a moment. "I do not understand it. What has been written within the Ledger is not only what I wrote but something else about him has been added in, on an entirely separate page, I might add."

Bridget's anger faded, her breath twisting about in her chest.

"What is it that has been said?"

Lady Yardley shook her head and then, without a word, handed "The London Ledger" to Bridget, who took her time, looking over the pages until she found his name.

"'*What may not be known to all of society is that Lord Landon holds his title but with heavy shadows behind it,*'" she read aloud. "'*Could this seemingly trusted gentleman be hiding something more? Something dark and unspoken which he has held to himself for so long, it would be a shock to everyone to know how well he has hidden it.*'"

Confused by what those words meant, Bridget looked straight back at Lady Yardley.

"I do not know what any of this is meant to imply."

"Nor do I." Miss Millington held out both hands as Lady Almeria shrugged. "But it certainly sounds very sinister. It suggests that Lord Landon is not all he appears to be, as though he holds or guards some great secret."

"It is not the sort of thing I have ever written in 'The London Ledger'. I have never allowed unsubstantiated rumor to be printed in 'The London Ledger' without explanation." Lady Yardley pressed her lips together, her cheeks stabbed with color. "I have always made certain that whatever I write or permit to be written is clear and concise. There have been times I have needed to include a rumor or whisper, certainly, but I have always made sure that they are written as such. I have never once written anything of a falsehood." She shook her head sharply. "I am greatly distressed by this, and cannot understand how it happened." Taking a breath, she settled her hand on Bridget's arm. "I apologize for my anger."

Bridget blinked, rapidly recalling what had occurred on the day that she had taken the pages to the publisher for Lady Yardley. At the time, she and her footman had both believed that it was nothing more than an accident – someone who had been running at such a pace that he had knocked into Bridget without even noticing her. He certainly had not stopped either, but mayhap that had been deliberate.

"I may... I may now know how this happened." Heat burned in her faces, as Lady Almeria and Miss Millington turned their attention to her. "Please understand. This was never done deliberately on my part."

"I believe you." Lady Yardley smiled briefly, then shook

her head, her eyes dropping to the ground for a moment. "I should not have spoken to you so sharply. I should not have believed you were to blame. It was my first instinct, but my first instinct is often wrong. I pray you will forgive me for that."

Bridget offered a small smile in return.

"Of course." Her anger faded away entirely, blowing into nothingness. "I quite understand. Please, allow me to explain." Taking a breath, she closed her eyes for a moment, remembering. "The carriage had stopped. My footman had offered to take the pages for me, but I had refused. I could see the publishers and therefore thought that there would be no difficulty in making my way there, even without my maid."

"It is not a disreputable area of town." Lady Yardley spoke quickly as Bridget nodded her head. "You would have been quite safe."

"Yes, of course – I believe that my footman was considering my lack of accompaniment." She shrugged her shoulders. "I continued to walk and suddenly something – or, I should say, someone – pushed into me very hard indeed. I was flung against one of the stone walls of a shop, striking my head and scraping my knuckles. The papers, of course, went everywhere. My footman came to help me at once, intending to go after whoever it had been, but the man had already run away."

"And did he see who this person was?" Miss Millington sounded deeply concerned. "You say he did not stop to even check if you were all right?"

"No, the footman did not see his face. This person ran directly into my path and, thereafter, fled... and the papers went everywhere." Bridget saw light began to dawn in Lady Yardley's eyes. Evidently, she had come to the same conclusion as Bridget herself. "The footman insisted that he would take the papers to the publishers, having first accompanied me back to the carriage. My head was aching so terribly, I agreed at once. He took them, explained what had happened, and returned to tell me that all was well." She flung out her hands. "I thought nothing more of it."

"You are not overly injured."

Lady Yardley was clearly concerned for her, and Bridget smiled, despite her current worry over what had taken place, and what she now realized about it.

"I had a slight bruise to my head and some scraped knuckles, that is all."

"But I do not understand." Lady Almeria spoke slowly, her eyes trained on Bridget. "Aid me, if you might. Is it that you believe the person who knocked into you did so purposefully?"

"That would be my first thought, yes." Bridget gestured to 'The London Ledger'. "That is the only way that papers could have been changed. The only way that this other passage which has been written about Lord Landon could have been placed within."

"I see." Lady Almeria frowned as Miss Millington shook her head in obvious dismay. "Someone has gone to great lengths then, to make certain that Lord Landon's name is smeared, without ever revealing their true selves."

"And also, in attempting to make me appear as though *I* am the one responsible." Lady Yardley sighed. "The rest of what has been written on that particular page is nothing but nonsense, notes about bonnets and filled with names which are entirely fictional. Most will not focus on those things but will, instead, read the part about Lord Landon, for it is the only thing on that page which makes sense."

Bridget drew in a sharp breath, something spiraling in her mind.

"It does mean also that whoever knocked into me had been waiting for someone to appear."

Lady Yardley nodded.

"Yes, it does." Her expression was dark, her tone grim. "I suppose that, to anyone paying attention, it would be expected that I would publish another Ledger very soon... and thus, this person was clearly waiting for me." She looked to Bridget. "I am truly sorry that *you* were the one who was injured, Miss Wynch. It ought to have been me."

"I was not injured," Bridget reassured her. "I was, perhaps a little taken by surprise, but suffered nothing of any long-term injury. I am sorry, however, that this occurred, and I did not tell you. Truly, I did not think anything like this would happen."

"Of course you did not." Lady Yardley put a comforting hand on her shoulder. "We must be on our guard. There is a reason for this – for *all* of this, although, of course, I could not say exactly what it is. But Lord Landon appears to have made an enemy who hides in the shadows. I shall have to speak to him also, of course."

As she glanced around the room, Bridget's stomach roiled, causing heat to begin to build.

"He will demand to know who wrote the other paragraph about him." Closing her eyes for a moment, she took a breath, then looked at Lady Yardley, her voice a little unsteady as she spoke. "He will want to know who wrote about such things about his interest in matrimony."

"He may not do so." Lady Yardley dropped her hand to her side. "And even if he should ask, there is no reason for me to inform him of who it was who wished for it to be written. Do not be concerned, Miss Wynch. I always take full

responsibility for what is written in the Ledger and therefore, should anyone question anything, the blame rests
solely upon me."

This offered a little relief to Bridget, and she took it,
mentally, with both hands, grasping at it tightly and
allowing it to chase away some of her fear.

"I see."

Her eyes snagged on a gentleman as she turned her
head away – a gentleman who was now reading the very
same Ledger that Lady Yardley held in her hand. Heat
began to prickle uncomfortably over her skin as Lord
Landon pushed one hand directly through his hair, then
shook his head furiously.

"I do not think we shall have to wait for his response."
Her voice was quiet; soft and filled with apprehension.
"Lord Landon is reading it now."

CHAPTER SEVEN

"My Lord?"

Heath resisted the urge to bark an order that he did not want to see any visitors this afternoon, looking up just as Lord Atherton strode into the room. He sighed heavily, rolling his eyes at his friend.

"If you are come to make certain that I am well, and not in any great state of despondency, you need not concern yourself."

"Landon." Lord Atherton inclined his head as stood near the door. "Yes, that is precisely why I am here. If you do not wish for company, however, then I –"

"I am just about to take my leave, Atherton." Heath gestured to the door. "You may join me if you wish."

He could not begrudge his friend his company, given he had come to make certain that Heath was quite well.

"Might I ask where it is you are going?"

Heath shrugged.

"Nowhere of any particular interest. I have visited an orphanage lately and intend to spend a little more time there. I am taking a donation with me this time."

To his relief, Lord Atherton said nothing. Instead, he simply nodded, meaning that Heath did not have to explain himself. Walking out of his study, Heath considered that, even if Lord Atherton *had* asked a good many questions, he had no intention of answering them, given that his mind kept turning over what had been written in the Ledger yesterday. What was it that would come to him? What consequences were to follow? His thoughts were many and terrifying, and the only way to escape from them was to think about what *else* he might do with his time. The thought of social activity was not a pleasant one for, in the midst of such events, could his enemy not be watching him, waiting for him, laughing silently at how much he intended to place upon Heath's shoulders at a moment of his choosing?

"Which orphanage, might I ask?"

Heath cleared his throat.

"Dove Street Orphanage."

Making his way towards the front door, he caught Lord Atherton's frown but did not respond to it. He had thought about going to another place but had instead decided to return to Dove Street, hoping Miss Wynch would not be present. She was still very much in his thoughts, given how much he regretted leaving her to one side for the moment. Seeing her at the orphanage had only made him appreciate her all the more. He admired her, his heart pulled towards her as though desperate to be near the lady, but he had forcibly dismissed it all. He could not allow himself to think of any young lady, not when there were such difficulties as these binding him to keep to himself, tying him to the past.

"I am also to stop at the poorhouse." Walking directly to the carriage, Heath glanced over his shoulder to Lord Atherton. "And at the hospital."

"It seems as though you are seeking some sort of salvation." The moment they sat in the carriage, Lord Atherton's questions began. "Surely you cannot be doing this after what was in the Ledger? I am sure all society will not believe a word of it."

Heath shook his head.

"I am not as convinced as you." His jaw flexed as he turned his head resolutely to look out the window. "It is just something I must do."

"If you indeed wish to aid those around you, then I admire you for it."

Lord Atherton's tone had grown a little quieter, reminding Heath of his friend's genuine concern.

"Then you must think of it only as charity, for I will not tell you much else." Keeping his gaze on the window. Heath did not so much as cast a glance over at his friend. "That is all that it is. Charity. I have a good deal and it is right for me to give some of it to those less fortunate."

"Certainly." Out of the corner of his eye, Heath saw the way that Lord Atherton leaned forward. "I am aware that you do not trust me, and I accept that, for it is entirely justified. However, I would ask you to consider what I will suggest: if you have any true difficulties, you must find someone to share your burden with, else you will collapse with the weight of it." He grimaced. "It does appear as though you are carrying some great trouble all of a sudden."

"That is because I am." Before he could prevent himself, the words slipped forth. "Yes Atherton, there is a great and heavy burden resting on my shoulders, but I certainly would not dare to speak of it to you."

Lord Atherton did not recoil, he did not frown, nor appear in any way upset. Instead, he merely spread his hands, his elbows resting lightly on his knees.

"As I have said, that is entirely understandable. But if it is to do with what has been written in 'The London Ledger', then might I suggest that you begin to loosen such a weight by speaking to the person who is responsible for the Ledger."

Heath considered for a moment, lifting his eyebrows as he turned back to face his friend. Lord Atherton's expression remained quite calm, although there was a hopeful glint in his eye.

"From what I understand, Lady Yardley does not write everything that goes in the Ledger."

"No, but she does read through it all and decides what shall be placed within it." Lord Atherton sat back in his seat as the carriage rumbled on. "If you seek to find someone responsible to speak with about what was placed in the Ledger, then she is the one you ought to speak with, in the first instance."

Heath bit his lip. What Lord Atherton did not know was the threat that had been made by the man who had pulled him into the dark alley that recent afternoon. Those threats seemed to align with what had been written in the Ledger. The words had been close to the truth but had not been it entirely. Were these the consequences he was meant to simply accept? Was there more to be said? Perhaps he should try to find out who had written that piece about him.

"There is the other paragraph also, although that, I suppose, can be easily explained."

Heath blinked.

"The other paragraph?"

"Yes, the one which suggests you are torn between finding a bride and wishing for your freedom." Lord Atherton chuckled softly. "No doubt some young lady of your acquaintance is eager to know precisely what your intentions are for the Season."

Instinctively, Heath's mind went directly to Miss Wynch. Could it be that she had been the one to write that paragraph, or had begged Lady Yardley to insert it in there? They were very well acquainted, he knew. Did *she* want to know what his intentions were for the Season? Was she desperate to understand exactly what it was that he was looking for?

Mayhap she was confused, although he certainly could not blame her for that, given how he had behaved thus far in their acquaintance. First, he had called upon her, only to have his visit last only a few minutes. Afterward, he had promised to call on her again but had never given her a time or even an expectation as to when it might take place. Despite his determination to stay away from her, no matter how hard he tried, he could not help but look at her, always catching her eye whenever they were in company together. It did not seem to matter where he stood, if she was present, their gazes would always meet. He had not asked her to dance again, not since they had danced the waltz, but his desire to do so again was very much present. No doubt she had heard of his desire to find a bride – a desire which was still there, especially when he thought of Miss Wynch. It was one he pushed aside, given these present circumstances, but now with the rumors floating around London about him, it would be little surprise if Miss Wynch was very confused indeed.

"You were thinking of someone, were you not?" Atherton chuckled as Heath's eyes flared wide, and grinned. "Miss Wynch, by any chance? Now, you need not look so surprised. It is not as though you have hidden your interest in her from anyone." Heath was about to state that he had no real interest in the lady, only to close his mouth firmly. He could not lie. "You have danced with her very often." Lord Atherton smiled, although there was no hint of teasing in his voice. "And you have called upon her once already, have you not?"

"She is not the only young lady I have called upon."

Lord Atherton laughed aloud.

"Good gracious, you do not need to defend yourself! There is nothing wrong with seeking out Miss Wynch, in finding her to be of great interest to you, and in spending as much time in her company as you can... though I suppose the latter is not something you are doing at present."

Heath's frown grew.

"And why would I not be?"

"Because you are taken up with whatever this other matter is." Lord Atherton lifted both hands defensively, stopping Heath's sharp response. "These last few days you have withdrawn from society. Yes, you have been present, but you have not danced, nor have you spoken to very many people. You have stayed at the edges – and now, I fear, will do so even more, after what has been written in the Ledger." Heath swallowed hard. He had wanted to behave as he normally would, had eagerly desired to dance – with Miss Wynch in particular – but his concerns had held him back. "Whatever it is that you are struggling with, you need not speak of it with me if you do not wish to. In fact," Lord Atherton chuckled, somewhat ruefully. "I would advise you *not* to do so. You may be vague, of course, but I can still be of aid to you without knowing the details of your situation. That is all I wish to offer you, Landon. I wish to provide support."

Considering this for a few moments, Heath pressed his

lips hard together. As yet, he had not spoken to anyone about his current difficulties, and it was becoming a rather heavy burden upon his heart and mind. Lord Atherton had obviously come to realize that he could not guarantee to hold his tongue and he was therefore unwilling to hear the intricacies of Heath's current struggles - but perhaps, Heath considered, there was a little that he could say, was there not?

Leaning his head back, Heath closed to eyes. Silence held his lips together for some moments until finally, he began to speak.

"There has been a threat made against me." Opening his eyes, he caught the way that Lord Atherton's eyes flared. "It is all very vague, but it hangs above me like a guillotine, threatening to slice down through me at any moment."

"And separate your head from your body?"

Lord Atherton's eyes had gone very wide indeed, and Heath shook his head.

"No, there is no immediate threat of death, if that is what you mean. What there is, however, is the threat of the loss of reputation and a great scandal that might have me cast from society. A scandal which would then pursue even my children, should there ever be any." Taking another breath, he shrugged. "And thus, I have chosen to step away from anyone I might come to care for." This was said without any particular detail, but with it being obvious that he spoke of Miss Wynch. Lord Atherton frowned but said nothing, his eyebrows low and his lips pursed. "I am uncertain as to what I am to do. Nothing specific has been said or done as yet, but I fear that this article in 'The London Ledger', this suggestion of some kind of guilt, is the beginning of what I am to face."

"But there is no truth in it." Lord Atherton dismissed it

with a wave of his hand. "What can the threat be? Someone has lied about you, but you will be able to prove your innocence one way or the other, I am sure."

At this, Heath winced, his stomach lurching.

"I cannot say much, my friend," he said heavily, passing one hand over his eyes. "But part of me believes that I deserve whatever consequences are to be brought to me."

His friend blinked back at him, only to then snort and throw up both hands.

"You must be jesting, surely? You do not deserve such threats."

"Perhaps I am not as blameless as you believe."

The carriage came to a stop and Heath shifted forward, preparing to step out as the footman hurried around to open the door. Lord Atherton shifted forward too, however, but swung his arm towards the door, holding it shut so that it could not be opened. His jaw was set, his eyes fixed as he looked at Heath with a steely gaze.

"Understand this, Landon, you are *not* a gentleman who deserves anything like what you have just described. All of us have made mistakes, certainly some more deliberately than others." He winced as Heath sat back against the squabs again. "There is not a single one of us who can hold ourselves higher than others and state that we do not regret anything which we have done. There is many a time when I have looked back on my life and lamented a great deal, but that does not mean that someone has any right to threaten me! That is *their* wrongdoing. I would not give you too much advice, but what I *would* say is to beg of you not to accept this as though it is your fate; something you must simply open yourself up to. There may be wrongdoing, certainly, but heavy dark consequences are not necessarily something you must just accept." Lord Atherton dropped his arm away from the door. "Even if you believe that you must, and have foolish expectations that it will somehow relieve your conscience."

Heath let out a slow breath, a little surprised at how much sense his friend spoke.

"I believe that you understand me more than I understand myself, Atherton." His smile was heavy. "I do feel as though I should permit these consequences to hold me. I know that I have done wrong."

Lord Atherton sat back in his chair as the footman waited patiently outside the carriage, ready to open the door whenever Heath indicated.

"You are a gentleman whom I consider to be one of the finest in all of London. It is not to say that you are incapable of doing wrong, but rather that I believe, knowing you as I do, that you will have done such a thing for some profound reason." He held out one hand, palm out to Heath. "Again, do not tell me what you have done, for I do not trust myself. I wish only to express to you that, if you have done something for good reason, I believe that is even less cause to accept dark and potentially dangerous consequences."

Heath dropped his head.

"It does not alleviate my guilt."

"Then that may be a burden which you will have to carry," Lord Atherton told him quietly, "but if there is such a severe threat as you express, then I beg of you to be cautious." With a quick smile, he folded his arms across his chest. "And I would tell you directly *not* to allow this danger to push you away from Miss Wynch. You have the opportunity for happiness, and it is not something many gentlemen are offered. To allow it to slip away would be possibly one of the most foolish things that you have ever done... and you are not known for foolishness."

Letting out a laugh that was somewhere between mirth and ruefulness, Heath gestured to the footman, who opened the door at once.

"You have more wisdom than I, and I thank you for it."

Lord Atherton chuckled.

"I do not think anyone has ever said such a thing to me before."

"I mean it, truly." Heath smiled at his friend. "Thank you for what you have said to me. It does give me some things to consider."

"I am glad."

Heath made to move to the now open door of the carriage, only for Lord Atherton to suddenly grasp his arm.

"Surely you cannot have *more* to say!"

Heath laughed, only for Lord Atherton to shake his head, his eyes holding fast to something outside of the carriage door.

"It seems as though something wishes you to greet Miss Wynch more suddenly than perhaps you are ready for." With a wry smile, he jerked his chin forward and Heath swiveled his eyes in the same direction. "It is almost as though she has been waiting for you."

Something balled in Heath's throat, something he forced himself to swallow away, for, standing in the doorway of the orphanage talking to Mrs. Martin, was Miss Wynch. As he watched, Mrs. Martin glanced towards them and before Heath could shrink back into the carriage, grinned widely, and gestured towards him, as Miss Wynch's eyes followed.

Their eyes met, and Heath's stomach twisted one way and then the other. Ice ran through his veins, followed by a furious fire that melted the cold away. Whatever was Mrs. Martin saying about him? No doubt she would already be telling Miss Wynch about his previous visit, which meant his attempt to stay away from Miss Wynch was going to be foiled.

"It seems as though fate is pushing me towards her."

As he muttered aloud to Lord Atherton, he caught his friend's broad grin.

"I quite agree," Lord Atherton chuckled, before gently pushing Heath in her direction. "On you go then. Let us see exactly what it is fate holds for you."

∼

"Miss Wynch."

Heath inclined his head. Miss Wynch smiled at him, but her smile did not linger, as though she were a little uncertain about his presence here.

"Mrs. Martin informs me that you have visited the orphanage before." She gave no murmur of greeting, only beginning to speak at once. "I did not know."

"I did not want to disturb you on my last visit." Even to his ears, the excuse sounded rather foolish. "Though I heartily congratulate you on the time you give to these children."

A flicker darted through her eyes.

"I give very little." She dropped her gaze. "Even in my circumstances, I recognize how much I have compared to their struggles." Heath nodded, guilt striking hard against his heart. He had not come here with the same motivations, but yet he ought to have done. She was everything he ought to have been. He resolved wholeheartedly to give of himself without any other motivation and to care for those who had so little. "Oh!" Miss Wynch's gaze went over Heath's shoulder, clearing a little in obvious surprise. "Good gracious,

Lord Atherton is here also." A small smile flickered back to her lips. "Perhaps you will bring all of the *ton* to join us here by the end of the Season."

"Mayhap. I will." Heath could not help but smile. "It would be a good resolution, do you not think?"

Much to his relief, Miss Wynch smiled brightly back at him.

"Certainly, it would be."

Mrs. Martin waved one hand in the general direction of the orphanage.

"I must return to my duties. Do come inside whenever you wish, Lord Landon. As always, we have been very glad to see you again, Miss Wynch."

"Do you come here alone?"

Heath looked first at Miss Wynch, then at the open door of the orphanage.

A slight blush touched her cheeks.

"I do." She lifted both shoulders. "My maid attends with me, of course."

Miss Wynch indicated the quiet girl who stood in the shadows of the doorway, patiently waiting for her. Heath offered Miss Wynch a small smile, his eyebrow arching.

"And might it be that your mother does not know where you are?"

Miss Wynch nodded.

"Nor does she care," came the somewhat harsh reply. "But I have my maid with me for propriety, of course."

"Of course."

They were then joined by Lord Atherton, who greeted the young lady but made no further comment. The grin on his face, however, spoke of a rather great delight in seeing Heath speaking to Miss Wynch, and he meandered away for a few moments, looking up at the orphanage.

"I have missed your company." Heath spoke rather more quietly to Miss Wynch, in the faint hope that Lord Atherton would not overhear him. "Forgive me for being so absent. I have had some... difficult circumstances."

For some moments, Miss Wynch did not say a single word. When she did, it was with a slight sigh that escaped from her first, before her smile returned.

"You are here now at least." Her gentle smile lifted his spirits a little. "And that will be enough for me. Oh! I have forgotten my reticule. I must go back in and find it. Please excuse me."

She turned to walk into the orphanage and Heath's heart lifted so high, it felt as though it might dance away from his chest. She was so very beautiful, her character so kind and generous, he did not think that he would find another young lady like her – not if he searched all of London for years upon end.

Miss Wynch had caught his attention at the first, simply because she was unlike any other young lady of his acquaintance. Now, however, she did so all the more - for what other young lady of London could he spy here? What other young lady was giving up her time for the poor and the unfortunate? No, Miss Wynch was unlike anyone he had never met, and he would be a fool to give her up. Lord Atherton was correct, and had spoken with more wisdom than Heath had ever credited him with. No matter what was to face him, he would have to find a way to listen to his heart and pray desperately that, whatever befell him, he could be honest with the lady. If she rejected him, as she would have every right to do, then he would not begrudge her that, but would still be glad that he had taken the chance, and had done all that he could to offer her his heart.

Otherwise, would he not live on in regret, wondering

whether or not she might have attached herself to him, even knowing the truth? With a set of his shoulders and a nod toward Lord Atherton, Heath made his way after Miss Wynch, quite certain now that he would not allow her free from his intentions again.

CHAPTER EIGHT

"I see that Lord Landon has made himself a little more inclined towards you these last few days."

Immediately heat flourished in Bridget's cheeks, but all the same, she nodded as Lady Cassandra and Lady Yardley smiled at her.

"It is very strange," Lady Yardley continued, as Bridget's gaze dropped back to her cup of tea. "I would have thought he might have appeared at my door by now, wanting to know where the article in the Ledger came from."

"I had considered that also," Bridget stated quietly. "I can give you no reason for why he has not come to call, however. He has not asked me of it either."

"But then again, he would not ask you." Lady Yardley reminded her quietly. "He does not know that you commissioned the other piece about him."

Something heavy dropped into Bridget's stomach.

"I suppose he does not."

She had quite forgotten that Lord Landon would not know that *she* had encouraged Lady Yardley to write the first article about him, wondering whether or not he would attach himself to a young lady this Season. Whenever they had been in company together these last few days, she had caught herself holding her breath, waiting for the moment when he might ask her about 'The London Ledger'. Thus far, of course, it had not come to pass – and perhaps would not at all.

"Do you care for him?"

Lady Cassandra's question was rather blunt, and Lady Yardley exclaimed so, but Bridget waved a hand.

"I do find it somewhat difficult to be open about my feelings, but I have no trouble in confessing to you both that yes, I find Lord Landon to be quite capable of stealing my heart." Her blush deepened, but she continued, for if she could not be honest with Lady Yardley and Lady Cassandra, then who could she speak openly with? "For whatever reason, writing that in the Ledger appears to have encouraged him in my direction. He has not spoken about any specific intentions as yet, but I am hopeful."

"As I believe you should be." Lady Yardley smiled warmly. "Good gracious, the gentleman has hardly been out of your company these last few days! He has been the first to seek out your dance card, the first to stand up with you, the first to make conversation with you. His attentions have been noticed, I am sure – and not just by myself."

Bridget dropped her gaze.

"My mother thinks nothing of it, for my sister continually whispers in her ear that nothing of any consequence will result." Shrugging lightly, she reached for her teacup once more. "I have a little more confidence, however."

"Which is just as it should be." With a firm nod, Lady Yardley gestured towards the cakes on the table. "Do you have something, my dear? I think –"

A knock at the door interrupted them. The butler came

in, announcing the arrival of none other than Lord Landon, expressing the fact that the gentleman wished to have a brief audience with Lady Yardley, even though the butler had informed him that she had a guest at present.

Immediately, Bridget's heart began to pound. Was it now that Lord Landon intended to come and speak of what had been in the Ledger? What a time he had chosen, a time when she was present!

"What say you?" Turning her head to Bridget, Lady Yardley held her gaze steadily. "It is a reasonable excuse to say that I have company, for that is precisely what I do have. I can easily send him away, asking him to call at another time."

Swallowing hard, Bridget took a breath.

"No, do not hold him back." Aware of the slight trembling in her limbs, she folded her hands in her lap, attempting to present the cool, calm demeanor which was surely expected. "So long as he does not mind my presence."

"Nor mine." Lady Cassandra threw Bridget an encouraging smile. "We need do nothing but listen, Bridget. That is all which will be required."

"Absolutely." Lady Yardley looked from one to the other before nodding to the butler. "Speak only if you wish, Bridget. If there is something that comes to your mind to say, have no hesitation, and be honest - for I believe that Lord Landon is looking for honesty and truth. I will give him as much of it as I can without informing him that you were the one who sent the papers to the publishers, unless, of course, you wish him to know that yourself."

Bridget pressed her lips tight together, closing her eyes for a second. There could be no harm in telling him what she had done, in taking the papers, or about what had happened thereafter. The only concern was that, surely, he then might surmise that, somehow, *she* had been the one to ask for the particular statement as regarded his intentions for the Season to be included.

But would that be so terrible a thing?

She had no opportunity to think on it further, for the door opened and Lord Landon stepped inside. They all rose to greet him. He showed no surprise upon seeing her, having evidently been informed by the butler that she was present.

"I am truly sorry for interrupting your conversation." He turned his attention directly to Lady Yardley. "I wish only for a brief audience with you, if I might."

Lady Yardley nodded and gestured for him to sit.

"But of course." The ladies resumed their seats, and Lord Landon settled opposite Lady Yardley. Bridget caught the faint look of surprise which filled his face. Perhaps he had expected Lady Yardley to ask Cassandra and Bridget to step out, or mayhap to suggest that they speak elsewhere, out of earshot of others. "You wish to speak about the Ledger, I understand."

Lord Landon's look of surprise only grew.

"Yes, I... How did you know?"

"It was not hard to surmise." Lady Yardley chuckled lightly. "There have been a couple of things written about you in the Ledger of late. The *ton* know that I am the one involved with the Ledger, and thus it seemed to me that you would wish to speak with me about it." Lord Landon nodded slowly. "However," Lady Yardley continued, quickly, "I should inform you that, while I know of the two articles which were published in 'The London Ledger', I myself was unaware of one of them until the printed paper was delivered to me."

"I see." Lord Landon nodded slowly, running one hand over his chin, perhaps wondering which one had been placed there without Lady Yardley's awareness. "The first does not overly concern me." Speaking slowly, he dropped his hand back to his lap. "It seems quite understandable that there are those within society who wish to know of my present intentions."

His head turned slightly, but before he could meet Bridget's gaze, she looked away, aware that the heat in her face had returned. She dare not look at him.

"It is the second one that concerns you, then."

"Yes." Lord Landon said, in answer to Lady Cassandra's question. "Someone has written something very dark about me, something which suggests that I may not be the gentleman I appear to be."

"Surely you believe that neither I nor any of those connected to the Ledger, would have permitted such a thing willingly?" Lady Yardley's voice was firm, her expression set. "I was utterly astonished when I saw what had been written there. I confess that I was rather angry at first, placing the blame on someone who was entirely innocent. Since then, it has been something of a puzzle to work out how it could have arrived within the Ledger, without my knowing of it."

"And have you reached any conclusions?"

Lady Yardley nodded.

"Yes, we have."

She did not give any further explanation, even though Lord Landon looked back expectantly. Instead, Lady Yardley looked first at Cassandra, then towards Bridget.

"Please." Lord Landon sat on the edge of his seat, his hands reaching forward. "Please, do tell me what your considerations are. They may be of help to me."

Lady Yardley sighed and shook her head.

"I am afraid I cannot give that to you."

She did not once look at Bridget, although Bridget knew all too well the reason that Lady Yardley remained silent was simply to protect her.

"Do you mean that you cannot tell me, or that you are choosing not to?"

Lady Yardley smiled quietly.

"It is because I can understand how such a thing has taken place, but I do not understand why or by whom."

"You will tell me no more than that?"

Bridget held her breath as Lady Yardley looked first to Lord Landon and then over to her.

"A person knocked the papers from the hands of my messenger who was delivering them to the publishers. My messenger was a little injured, but the person who ran into them was not recognized. That person ran off immediately, their face was not seen, and I can give you no description of them."

"It was me." The shock that overtook Lord Landon's expression was quickly reduced when Bridget hurriedly began to explain. "I do not mean to say that it was I who wrote such a dark thing about you in 'The London Ledger', more that I was the messenger on my way to deliver the pages to the publisher on Lady Yardley's behalf, only to be knocked aside by some fellow. The pages of the Ledger fell to the ground, scattered all about, and it must have been then that the additional paper was dropped amongst them and, thereafter, was included in the Ledger."

Lord Landon gave no response, other than to hold her gaze for some moments. Silence floated between them, and Bridget's heart began to quicken all the more, driven by the sudden fear that he was not about to accept her explanation.

"It was not Miss Wynch's fault." Lady Yardley's tone dropped a little, perhaps concerned that Lord Landon was about to blame her for something. "She did not see this person coming."

"No, of course not." Lord, Landon spoke quickly, attempting now to convince them all that he bore Bridget no ill. "Were you quite alright, Miss Wynch?"

She nodded.

"I banged my head a little, but it was not severe." She shook her head. "I am very sorry that such a thing occurred. However, I can promise you that it was not intentional. I did not notice anything happening to the pages when they fell, and my footman and I gathered them up and then delivered them as planned. Thus, when Lady Yardley brought what had occurred to me, I was just as shocked as she."

Lord Landon nodded and again rubbed his chin.

"And you say that you caught no glimpse of the person who knocked into you, the person who would have dropped this extra paper?"

Bridget shook her head.

"My coachman stated that it was a young man." She lifted both shoulders. "But aside from that, I can offer you nothing."

"And even that description would not be particularly helpful." Lady Yardley shook her head. "I believe that whoever planned such an endeavor would have done so without revealing themselves in any way."

Lord Landon's eyes widened a little.

"You mean to say, then, that you believe the person who knocked into Miss Wynch would not have been the person who wrote the article?"

"Certainly, I do believe that whoever wrote it would not

have been the one to 'deliver' it into the dropped papers."
Lady Yardley offered him a small, sad smile. "There have
been some dark times in my own life, Lord Landon, and
what I have learned is that those who do evil deeds often
hide themselves away, so that their cruelty will not be
revealed, or associated with them in any way."

Lord Landon let out a slow breath, grimacing as he
did so.

"It seems to be a wise thought."

"Might you have any idea as to who would wish to do
such a thing?"

The question was from her lips before Bridget could
prevent it but, to her relief, Lord Landon was quick to
answer her question.

"The truth is, I do believe that I might know who has
written such a thing about me." He let out such a heavy sigh
that Bridget's concern grew significantly. "What has been
said is not the truth in its entirety, I can assure you of that,
but there is some darkness in my past. Choices I have made,
things that I have done." Shrugging, he looked down at the
floor. "Mayhap I am not worthy of such censure, but I am
not stainless, and there may be a good reason for their
behavior."

"If someone has something against you, Lord Landon,
then it is their duty to bring it to you face to face, rather than
to whisper about you in the shadows."

Lady Yardley spoke quite calmly, and as Bridget
watched, she caught the small sad smile lifting Lord
Landon's lips.

"Well, such a thing may be true, but not everyone is
willing to do such things."

There was such a sadness about him that Bridget's heart
turned over for him. What was it he was enduring? What

was it that he spoke of in such a sorrowful manner? And why was there such a heaviness about his eyes? Was the person whom he believed had done this someone close to him?

"What will you do to try and make it right?" she found herself saying, sitting a little further forward in her chair as if she wanted to move closer to him. "Is there anything you can do?"

Taking a deep breath, Lord Landon spread his hands.

"There is not much that can be done. Nothing conclusive has been said but I have no doubt rumors will fly around about the *ton* now regardless." A slightly jarring laugh came from him. "After all, I have no doubt that someone in society will combine both the first thing that has been written about me with the second."

A little confused, Bridget held his gaze.

"Whatever do you mean?"

Lord Landon sighed and shrugged, pulling his gaze away from her now.

"Simply to say that someone, no doubt, will believe that my change of heart about my marriageable status is linked to the latter. Society will think some darkness has held me back from my initial plan to find a bride." His laugh was hoarse. "Mayhap some will congratulate themselves on staying far from me."

Immediately, Bridget closed her eyes. This had certainly not been her intention, for she had wanted only to find out precisely what it was that Lord Landon was thinking about his marriageable status. Now, it seemed, she had injured him in a manner that she had never intended.

"That may be so," Lady Yardley agreed, quietly. "I do hope that you understand that such a thing was not the intention of those who wished to have that paragraph placed within the Ledger."

She did not once look at Bridget as she spoke, but all the same, Bridget's face grew hot and she kept her gaze low, dropping her head a little further forward.

"I quite believe you." Lord Landon's voice was still rather heavy. "All the same, it is rather unfortunate." Nothing but silence followed his statement. Bridget licked her lips, aware of the growing desire to confess to him that *she* had done so, to explain to him why she had felt the urge to write such a thing within the Ledger. Before she could say anything more, however, Lord Landon rose abruptly to his feet. "I have kept you much too long from your conversation." He bowed to each of them in turn, an apology on his lips. "Forgive me, and thank you for being so very gracious with your explanations, Lady Yardley. It is greatly appreciated."

Bridget rose to her feet as Lady Yardley and Lady Cassandra did the same, ready to bid Lord Landon farewell. He looked at them all, his eyes gazed on hers for a little longer than to the others, and then he took his leave.

Bridget's feet moved of their own accord, hurrying her, urging her towards the door after him. She heard Lady Yardley's faint voice calling after her, but she did not stop. She *had* to say something, had to *do* something, had to tell him why she had been the one to write such a thing in the Ledger in the hope that he would forgive her for her foolishness.

"Lord Landon."

He turned to face her, surprise lifting his eyebrows.

"Miss Wynch?"

Bridget's mouth went dry, and she forgot completely

what it was that she was going to say. Beginning to stammer now, mortification burning through her, she shook her head.

"Are you quite alright?"

The door to the drawing room was still ajar, but Bridget moved quickly away from it, not wanting either Lady Yardley or Lady Cassandra to overhear her. Swallowing against the dryness in her throat, she approached Lord Landon.

"I... I confess to you that *I* was the one who asked for the article about your intentions to be placed within the Ledger." She could not look at him, her eyes darting away and then back toward his face. "I asked Lady Yardley to place the question as regards your marriage intentions. I did so because I wanted to know the truth. I wanted to understand where I stood and if I had...." Swallowing hard, she closed her eyes. "If I had any hope."

Lord Landon did not react with any sort of frustration. He did not frown, his eyes did not narrow either - instead, he simply nodded, his head dropping forward for a moment.

"I can understand why you did so." His tone was heavy and, when she dared to fix her gaze upon him, she was rather astonished at how sorrowful his expression was. "I have not treated you fairly. I apologize for that."

"I do not feel any irritation towards you." Again, her feet urged her closer, as though they were joined by an invisible thread that was tugging her ever closer. "If there is some trouble... some difficulty which I might help you with, I –"

"There are more difficulties than you may know." Lord Landon passed one hand over his eyes, but when he dropped it back to his side, his other hand reached to grasp hers for a moment. "But the truth is that I do not want to be apart from you. The reason I told a particular young lady that my friend was the cause of the rumors about my desire to marry is because I was afraid of what the situation might be for me... and, therefore, for whichever young lady I connected myself to."

Something gleamed in his eye and Bridget caught her breath. His intention, his attentions – attentions to her, had been genuine then. She had no doubt that he spoke of her without being overly specific.

"You pulled away out of concern."

Lord Landon nodded.

"I did. However, that does not mean that I was correct to do so. Perhaps I should have been forthcoming rather than withdrawing entirely." With a wry smile, he shrugged his shoulders, his hand squeezing hers as a soft heat began to build within her. This was a different sort of warmth, however. It was not one that came from embarrassment, but rather from the sheer joy of being close to him again. "I should like to talk with you, if I may." Lord Landon's smile began to crack. "Not here, of course, but at a time when you might be able to give me your full attention, when I might explain a particular matter to you." Taking a breath, he let it out and set his shoulders, causing a knot to form in Bridget's throat. "In truth, Miss Wynch, there is a threat upon me. A threat which, in many ways, I have brought upon myself, but it is there all the same. I will not pretend - my desire is, indeed, to further our connection, but I cannot do so knowing that what lingers near me may one day come to affect you also. Therefore, I would rather be honest with you about all of my present difficulties and where they have come from. If you choose to reject our acquaintance thereafter, I will be more than understanding."

"I am sure that I could do no such thing."

It might well have been his nearness to her, but for

whatever reason, her response came urgently. No, she could never pull herself away from Lord Landon, not when her heart leaped so furiously in her chest when he came near, not when her desire was to linger close to him.

"You have a great sweetness about you." Lord Landon's expression softened as he looked steadily into her eyes and, after a moment, his fingers sought to lace through hers. "I believe it is what drew me to you in the first place. Given the fact that you are so entirely unaffected, quite in contrast to so many other young ladies in London, and with such a delight about your character, it is astonishing to me that no gentleman has sought you for himself as yet." When had he moved closer? Bridget caught her breath, wishing desperately that she could find the same sort of compliment to offer him, the same sort of kindness in her own remarks about him, but instead all she could do was stare up into his eyes. "My interest in you is genuine." Lord Landon's voice was low, his head dropping just a little. "It has pained me to step away from you, albeit for a short time. How much I wish it were otherwise."

"You need not stay away from me."

Quite where such boldness had come from, Bridget did not know, but his increasing nearness was so overwhelming, it was as though her mouth spoke of the contents of her heart and the urgency of her desire without her having any control of it. Lord Landon's eyes flickered again. He moved closer, so that their bodies almost touched, only for him to then turn away sharply. His hand dropped from her and, try as she might, Bridget could not help the gasp of disappointment which broke from her lips.

"Forgive me." Shaking his head, he ran one hand over his forehead, no longer looking at her. Bridget's heart began to cry out immediately, wanting desperately to rush forward, to throw herself into his arms, to beg him not to step away from her so soon, not when he had ignited such feelings within her. Instead, she simply stood still. "As I have said, there is much which I must tell you first." Lord Landon's voice was soft, yet determined. "As I told you, there is some truth in what has been written in the Ledger, which is why I am so very concerned. If the truth is known, if it is revealed, then..."

Still rather befuddled by the great rush of overwhelming feelings which now tore through her, Bridget dragged in a long breath in an attempt to steady the shaking which was now racing through her very soul.

"What is the truth, Lord Landon?" Her voice was trembling now, but a steady determination began to grow. "You cannot draw so close to me. You cannot offer me the hint of a promise, only to then withdraw – whatever your reasons for doing so!"

Lord Landon let out a slow breath and closed his eyes. Spreading out his hands, he looked at her again.

"I must explain all to you," he began, reaching to take her hand again. "I have never said a word of this to anyone. I have not even told Lord Atherton, even though he is my closest friend. I will tell you the truth, even though it must be explained, in the hope that you will understand my concern and my reasons for my actions."

Bridget lifted her chin, fixing him with her gaze, quite certain that nothing he could say would turn her away from him.

"Then please tell me."

Again, Lord Landon took a breath, closed his eyes, and allowed his fingers to twine around hers. Then he told her the truth in one simple sentence.

"I stole the title from my twin brother."

CHAPTER NINE

Try as he might, Heath could not get Miss Wynch's look of utter shock out of his mind.

She had stood there in stunned silence for many minutes and, even when he had spoken her name, she had not immediately responded. He had not meant to inform her of what he had done standing in Lady Yardley's hallway, but it had sprung from his lips without any real thought of what it would mean, thereafter. He had wanted to explain, had wanted to tell her all, but at that very moment, Lady Yardley had stepped out into the hallway and encouraged Miss Wynch back into the drawing room. After all, it would not be proper for them to be standing alone any longer, she had reminded them both with a smile - a smile that neither Heath nor Miss Wynch had managed to return.

Now here he was in Lord Maddock's ballroom, having attended in the hope of seeing and speaking to Miss Wynch but, thus far, she had not made a single appearance. He had no idea what her reaction would be to his confession, other than that initial shock. There had not been time to give her any explanation, of how it had happened, or of what had been the situation, the circumstances, and therefore he could not give her any reason for why he had done such a thing. Did she think that he had done it out of pure selfishness? Did she believe him an arrogant sort? They did not know each other particularly well as yet, he supposed. Had it been worth the risk?

Muttering to himself he shook his head rather wryly.

"I knew there was a chance that she would turn her back on me."

"Are you murmuring to yourself, or do you have some very small companion near you?"

Heath started in surprise, only to roll his eyes at Lord Atherton.

"I have no difficulty in admitting that I was speaking only to myself." He shrugged as his friend lifted a questioning eyebrow. "I have taken some of your advice. You may be astonished, I am sure, but I have decided that when it comes to Miss Wynch, I am not about to give her up."

"I am very pleased to hear it."

"My determination does not mean that she will feel the same, however." Speaking a little ruefully, Heath let out a heavy sigh. "Indeed, in speaking to myself, I am reminding myself that *this* was the choice I made, the risk I took."

A slight look of puzzlement crossed Lord Atherton's face as he frowned, his eyes searching Heath's, features.

"What risk do you speak of?"

"I told her the truth." Heath scowled as Lord Atherton's puzzled frown remained. "It is a truth I am unable to share with you, as you yourself have suggested, but it does mean that she might very well decide to step away from me. I would not blame her if she wished to do so, for I am not, perhaps, the gentleman she expected."

"You would have to be a very flawed gentleman indeed if that were the case." Lord Atherton smiled warmly as Heath threw him a quick grin.

"You are always coming to my defense." Shaking his head. Heath put one hand on Lord Atherton's shoulder. "And I appreciate that."

"Lord Landon."

As Heath turned, he noted Lord Atherton immediately melting away and knew instantly who it was that approached him, even before he caught her gaze. His heart swelled with relief, only to jerk with a sudden fear that she had come to speak with him only to tell him that she no longer wanted to be in his company.

"Miss Wynch." He bowed and Miss Wynch lowered her gaze as she bobbed a curtsey. She did not lift it again and, instantly, Heath's stomach dropped to the floor, his hopes shattering. Was this to be the end of their acquaintance? "I suppose I must have shocked you greatly." Thinking that there was no real reason to pretend otherwise, Heath spoke with great haste. "You will, no doubt, be utterly confounded by what you have heard from me. There is an explanation of course, but it is entirely up to you whether or not you wish to hear it."

There was a long silence. Miss Wynch kept her gaze low and did not look at him. Even as a small sigh broke from her mouth, she did not lift her head.

"My instinct tells me to walk away from you, Lord Landon." Finally, her eyes lifted, her lip caught between her teeth for a moment. "But I believe that you deserve the opportunity to explain yourself. And I will admit to bearing some curiosity about how such a thing as you say you have done could even be possible."

Heath let out a long slow breath, closing his eyes and

finding himself so overwhelmed that it took some moments to compose himself.

"I do not think I could explain just how much I appreciate this." Aware of the gruffness of his voice, he shook his head. "There are a good many things that have offered consequences in my life. Some have been of my own doing, some have come from other sources, but in this particular case, it is certainly my own fault." Miss Wynch continued to look at him and Heath resisted the urge to touch her hand. "Do you think that you might allow me to explain all of it to you, here?"

Miss Wynch bit her lip, then nodded.

"I suppose very few people would miss me. Should we find a quiet corner to sit in?" Caught again by relief, Heath nodded, his throat tight. Miss Wynch glanced up, then smiled at him, although it was still a little sad, a little restrained. "Yet again, you find that my mother cares very little about what I am doing at present, although perhaps in this case that is to my advantage."

Heath laughed softly.

"To *our* advantage, Miss Wynch." He hesitated, looking around the room. Should he take her to a quiet corner of the room, as she had suggested? They could certainly find a place to converse, although no doubt someone would take notice of him and his particular attentions to the lady. Was that something he would be quite contented with? Miss Wynch was looking at him, her gaze steady, her expression calm and yet, Heath himself felt nothing but swirling anxiety over how he would explain himself, and whether or not she would accept him. His heart lurched at the idea that she might step away from him, but he did not allow himself to linger on that thought. "Would you take my arm?"

When he offered it to her and she accepted, placing her

hand upon it, Heath's heart roared with such a fury that it was as though it feared that this was the last time that she would ever be so close to him. Thus, he allowed himself a little more time to find a suitable place, walking slowly as they meandered around the room. He could say nothing, do nothing other than think of her – think of how separated they might become in the times hereafter... and it would all be his own fault.

"Shall we have a seat here?" Seeing two vacant chairs, isolated in the shadowy corner of the room, Heath gestured towards them and, seeing her nod, led her to them. The rest of the room was in joyous occupation, and he felt as though his heart were being pulled from his chest. He had never told anyone what had taken place so many years ago, and even now confessed himself to be somewhat afraid of doing so. What if she were to push him aside? What if she told others? Again, Heath reminded himself that consequences *might* occur, but he had no choice but to accept them, and yet, as he looked into her eyes, the desire to tell her everything was severely lacking. Despite that, he forced himself to speak.

"I have never told anyone about what I have done." Taking a breath, Heath looked down at the floor. "I will begin by stating that I am deeply ashamed of my actions. I justified them to myself, stating that they were for the best and, I confess, in many ways, I still believe that." He saw her eyebrows lift, her blue eyes widen, and his stomach turned this way and that, as though he were in the middle of a stormy sea being tossed all about. "My actions came from a place of concern." Even saying such things made him sound like a charlatan, and he shook his head. "Forgive me, it is not to say that I have any excuse for doing as I did. I could have gone about it an entirely different way, but at the time, I saw no other way to fix the problem. While I did worry about the situation as regarded my family, I should not have been deceitful."

"What precisely is it that you did?"

Swallowing against the tightness in his throat, Heath fought to find the words to answer her question clearly.

"My brother and I are twins. He was the one born first, but by only a few minutes – but that is a fact that I only discovered when my father was dying. My father always refused to tell us which of us had been born first – insisting that he would not reveal that until he was on his deathbed. He also insisted that we both receive the same education, such that either one of us might successfully take on the weight of the title when the time came. I wondered if my father would tell the truth about our birth – for the midwife had died not long after we were born, and no one else knew who was first – or whether he would choose whoever he thought best suited at the point when he was dying, and declare that they had been first born, regardless of the true order of birth which should have determined his heir. Unfortunately, my brother – Lord Barrett Northdale - has always been something of a reprobate. He hated my father's attitude and refused to learn what he should have, about managing the estates and the like. Instead, he turned to self-indulgence." Sighing, Heath lifted his head a little, grief striking hard at his heart. "When our mother died, he was entirely absent and then, when my father became ill shortly afterward, he did not show his face. I'd heard nothing from him for around three years by this point – all I'd heard were the rumors and whispers which spun themselves around our family name. I was horrified to hear of how he was choosing to live and, in that situation, it was then that I acted."

"Goodness." Miss Wynch's eyes were swirling with shades of green and blue. "I am sorry that you had so much to deal with alone."

Heath nodded, struggling to hold her gaze. He took another breath, having not expected this to be as difficult to speak of as it was proving to be.

"My father was very ill, as I have said, and it became clear that he was not going to live for much longer. Thus I sought to find my brother. I sent many men out to find him, but he did not arrive home and could not be found – even the rumors of his actions had ceased. The whole household was in utter agony, wondering where my brother was – I sent letter after letter to as many places as I could think of, begging him to return to our father's bedside in time. You can imagine my difficulty, I hope. I had a brother who was absent from the house, I had a father who was begging for his sons to be near him so that he might pass on his last few words to us both. Instead, he only had me."

"Oh, that is terrible!"

Swallowing again, he dragged air into aching lungs.

"When my father asked for his will to be brought, I knew that it was time."

His whole body trembled as he spoke as if it were finally freeing itself of the guilt that he had been hiding from everyone else for so long. It was almost a catharsis to be able to speak so, to be able to be honest and open without any sense of foreboding. Yes, she might turn away from him, yes, she might decide that he was not worthy of her, but at least he would have been honest. At least he would have spoken with as much truth as he could, telling her what he had chosen to do, to save his family name. What Miss Wynch would do thereafter was entirely up to her.

"You did something with his will, then?"

Heath licked his lips.

"Not exactly. When our man of business delivered the Will to Landon Park, there was something else with it – a sealed envelope, which had been sealed on the day we were born, and never opened since. As I described, my father had always said that he would only tell us who had been born first when the time of his death came, and I looked at that envelope with a dawning recognition that it most likely contained that information, written down by the midwife at the time of our birth. When the Will and the envelope arrived, I confess that I looked at them before giving them to my father. What shocked me was that, within that envelope, there were two sheets of paper – one declared my brother first born, the other declared me to be so. You can imagine my horror upon seeing that, for it meant that my father had intentionally planned, even from our birth, to potentially break the laws under which titles are inherited. His Will was no better, for it laid many things out, but there were spaces left, where he might write in the names, as he chose. I took the Will and the envelope to him, and demanded an explanation."

"Oh my! What did he say?"

Shaking his head, he took a deep breath.

"He defended his actions, saying that he had hoped that we would both be men well able to be Earl, and that he had also done it in case one of us died in an accident, before he died himself. It seemed sensible, but it had done terrible things to both Barrett and I, changing the course of our lives. I demanded, then, that he tell me the truth, tell me which of us had actually been born first and, in the end, he told me."

She took a sharp breath, her eyes fixed on him.

"And what did he declare to be the truth?"

"That Barrett was born first. You can imagine my horror upon hearing that – for my brother is a man less suited to the responsibilities of a title than anyone else I had ever met. In short, Miss Wynch, I then convinced my father, as he lay on his death bed, to burn the paper from the envelope which named Barrett as firstborn, keeping only the paper which named me so, and to fill in the names in those spaces in his will, to put my name as the one who would inherit most of the properties, as well, although my brother still inherited some – quite enough to support himself. Because of my efforts, my father kept the paper that lied and burned the one which was the truth. He wrote my name in my brother's place, and my brother's in mine, in his Will, and thereafter, upon his death, I took on the responsibilities which came with the title of Earl of Landon. In due course, I was confirmed in the title, and took my place in the House of Lords." Breathing heavily now, he shook his head, ravaged by both guilt and relief. "I see now that I should have spoken to my brother - over the years I should have had many a conversation with him, long before my father's last hours, rather than do as I did - and I understand that it may cause you great distress to hear how I chose to act – but it is what I did, and I will admit to it. I did it for the sake of my family, and all of our tenants, for they would have suffered under my brother's hand. Believe me, Miss Wynch, it is not something that I am proud of. My choice is not something which has ever filled me with joyous delight, but I have convinced myself, repeatedly, that it was for the good of my family."

There was a prolonged time of silence, a moment when Heath swallowed hard, forced his mouth closed, and waited for her to respond. There was no smile on her face. There was no look of contentment nor understanding. Instead, she simply looked back at him as though he were explaining some great mystery to her; a mystery which, as yet, she could not fully comprehend. How much Heath wished he could see into her thoughts! How much he wished that he could understand all that she thought and felt about him at present. Little doubt it would be rather distressing to know such a thing, but all the same, the silence was a torment.

"Might I ask something?" Miss Wynch spoke softly. "Might I ask if your brother knows of this?"

"If he knows of my deception?" Heath lifted one shoulder, his hands on either side of him. "It is rather difficult for me to say. I am not entirely certain, for it is not something that we have ever discussed. It may sound very strange to you, but it appears to be a situation that we have both simply accepted. Perhaps because he has assumed that what my father revealed was that I was the firstborn, and he has not questioned it? No doubt my brother hides his true feelings from me in that regard, for I do not know whether he held, under his show of dissipation, a desire to be Earl, and we have never discussed it, it is not something we have ever brought to the fore. The only thing he has commented on is how free he is at present, how little he cares about the title, and how much he is relieved that he has no responsibilities." Again, Heath shrugged both shoulders, looking away from her. "I do not know if it is how he truly feels, however. And again, this is not to say that I have any excuse for what I did, Miss Wynch. I do not think of myself as some good soul who has done precisely what they ought about my family situation. I have struggled with my actions for many years, questioning whether or not I did the right thing. Even now, I recognize that my desire to do good works amongst the poor and those less fortunate is, in part at least, done to ease my conscience."

He saw her eyes flare and pulled his gaze away from her, all the more embarrassed.

"You mean to say that your presence in the orphanage came simply from a desire to ease your shame?"

His stomach tight and tense, Heath nodded.

"It would do me no good to pretend otherwise," he told her softly. "I might state that no, I came solely out of my own desire to help those who have little compared to myself, but it would not be true. Although I rapidly recognized this, and chose to do more, for the sake of helping people. Even at my estate, I have always made certain to care for those who have less. It is one of my duties, certainly, but it does help to ease one's guilt." He smiled rather ruefully. "The only thing I can do in such regard is to ask you for your forgiveness for hiding my character from you."

"You have not told a single soul about what you have done, save for myself?" Miss Wynch frowned as Heath nodded. "And yet you feel the need to absolve yourself before me?"

"I do so because of what I feel." Choosing not to continue justifying himself, given that he had said everything else there was to say, Heath practically threw himself upon her mercy, his heart pouring out all that was within it. "Mayhap you will think me foolish. Mayhap you will laugh at my desperate hopes, but I *have* come to care for you, Miss Wynch. We may not know each other particularly well as yet, but I know enough to understand how much my heart has become involved. There is more to say on that matter, more to understand, but the thought of allowing myself to pursue you without you knowing the truth was something I could not permit."

She regarded him, her eyes a little wider than before, her lips trembling slightly. Heath still had very little idea of what she would say, or how she would respond, for her expression gave very little away, save for the fact that she was rather overcome.

"I shall not say that what you did was right." Miss Wynch took in a long breath, her voice low, her brow furrowed. "But I can neither congratulate nor condemn you for it. I understand the responsibilities which come with bearing a title. To fear that nothing but shame and ruin would come upon your family, should your brother be first-born, must have been a significant weight indeed."

"It was – but again, I do not use it to excuse myself. I have spent many years bearing the weight of my conscience. No doubt it will be my burden for the rest of my days - the load I have chosen to place around my own neck." Heath flung up both hands, his gaze now dropping away from her face. "I will never pretend that my actions were right. I will never believe that my reasons for doing so were completely justified. I am beyond that. I accept my wrongdoing, but yet it cannot be changed. It is not something that can ever be resolved. I carry the title, and once a man is confirmed into the title, that cannot be rescinded, so I must bear the responsibility even while I bear the shame of claiming it for myself."

When Heath looked at Miss Wynch again, she was the picture of confusion. Her gaze was now fixed on something across the room as she chewed the edge of her lip. Her brow was gently lined, the corners of her eyes flickering with consideration as she let out a long, slow breath.

"You say that your brother has never known of this? Has never asked for any more detail of what happened at the time of your father's death?" Her eyes slid to his. "Might I ask if he has ever shown any inclination towards desiring the title, even in these later years since your father's passing?"

Heath shook his head.

"Quite the opposite, in fact. He has always expressed relief that he has not had to carry the same burdens as I." A lump settled in his throat. "Barrett did not return home until three months after our father's passing. He was not there for the funeral and did not observe the mourning period. These last two years he has been a little more inclined towards gentlemanly behavior, showing some degree of responsibility ever since he has been wed, but even now, on the rare occasions when we meet, he seems to delight in how little he has to care for."

Speaking honestly, without a single lie crossing his lips, Heath allowed his gaze to meld to hers.

"Might I ask if you have considered that what was written in the Ledger might have come from your brother?"

Heath smiled grimly.

"It has been a consideration of mine, certainly." Taking another breath, he shrugged. "In addition, I was accosted by a particular fellow a short while before what was written in 'The London Ledger' appeared. I do not know his name, nor could I recognize his face. In short, however, he threatened me, making it clear that there would be consequences for some previous wrongdoing that I had committed. He told me that he knew what I had done, and thus I have now been expecting something heavy to fall around my ears. I do not know precisely what it will be, but I am certain it is related to what I have done to my brother."

To his utter astonishment, Miss Wynch leaned forward at once and settled her hand on his. Her eyes were furiously searching his face, her cheeks draining of color.

"Do you think he means to harm you?"

"I cannot be sure. When it does come, I have every hope that it will not be of any great severity."

His smile was still rather tight, though he turned his hand so that their fingers interlaced. Dare he allow himself to hope? Dare he allow himself to believe that she would not abandon him, would not turn her back on him, even though he had told her the very worst of himself?

"Oh, you must be careful." She caught her breath suddenly, one hand flying to her mouth. "This is why you told Lady Margaret that you had no intention of seeking a bride, is it not? Your intentions changed because of this threat."

"Yes," Heath said nothing more, seeing her eyes close as she finally drew to an understanding. "I am sorry that there was such confusion, but I told myself I was foolish to even *think* of considering a bride when I had such guilt upon me, such danger near to me." Raking one hand through his hair, he shook his head. "My attempts to resolve it have been selfish, while you are nothing but unselfish, Miss Wynch. You give your time and even your very self to those less fortunate, simply because you see the need there and you want to fulfill it. I sought to do so, at first, only for myself. I have been wrong in a good many things, but I have told you all now, so that, should you dare to permit yourself to consider me, you will know everything. You will know the burden which weighs up on my shoulders and which will continually settle there, no matter how long I live."

Miss Wynch opened her eyes. Her hand squeezed his.

"Of course I consider you still." Her smile caught him unawares, and now it was him who sucked in air to tight, trapped lungs. "You may carry this burden for the rest of your days, but it can be lightened. Perhaps you should consider telling your brother the truth, telling him of what you have done, in much the same way as you have told me." Heath blinked rapidly, surprise flooding through his chest, forcing his eyes wide. He had never once considered doing such a thing, for even the mere *hint* of that idea had been enough for him to fling it far away. He could never tell his brother the truth, could he? "If it is your brother who is threatening you, then perhaps all it requires is a confession," Miss Wynch continued softly. "Mayhap he has heard something from someone connected with your father's man of business – some passing comment about that envelope which was sent with the Will - and now desires simply to know the truth from you. You yourself said that he has become a little more responsible of late. Perhaps that responsibility has given him time to consider, and mayhap his consideration is now the reason you find yourself in such difficulties."

Her thoughts on the matter were so startling and yet so wonderful, Heath did not quite know how to respond. He simply stared at her, looking at her with wide eyes, confused and frustrated at his own lack of wisdom in such matters, but all the more grateful for hers.

"I am glad that I have never told anyone of my trials before, Miss Wynch." Her frown threatened to return but he managed a small chuckle. "I say that only because I believe that I have found the right person to speak to. Your wisdom in this is profound. I cannot believe that I would have been offered the same prudent counsel had it been someone else I had spoken to." His smile curved a little more. "Particularly had it been Lord Atherton."

At this, Miss Wynch let out a small laugh, and Heath found himself smiling at her. There was such a relief in his soul, it felt as though he were no longer being crushed by an invisible weight. Yes, the shame still lingered, and certainly, his guilt was not to be escaped, but the sheer relief which came from knowing that Miss Wynch was not about to turn from him was almost more than he could bear. How much he longed to take her in his arms, to tell her the true depths of all that he felt, to tell her how much she overpowered him simply by being so near! But he restrained himself, letting his thumb run over the back of her hand as their fingers remained joined, and she looked into his face with a tenderness that Heath had never expected.

"I should not linger too long." As irritating as it was, Heath knew that he had to consider what others might be seeing. "I should like to court you, Miss Wynch. I should like all of the *ton* to know that you are the one I have settled my intentions upon." Miss Wynch's smile only grew, offering Heath all the more encouragement. "I shall speak to your father... that is, only if you wish me to do so. I have no intention of courting you and then throwing you aside for someone else. When I ask to court you, it is with the belief and the hope that my future will be with you." There was no sudden gasp of astonishment, no flaring of her eyes or tears dripping onto her cheeks. Instead, she simply nodded. No words were spoken between them, but the understanding was so great, it was all Heath could do to remain in his chair. "Then might I have your waltz this evening, Miss Wynch?"

He had not dared ask her before now before they had spoken, but he could no longer hold back. The urge to have her in his arms was much too great.

"Of course you may." She handed him her dance card without hesitation. "And should you permit me, I would like to aid you as you search for your brother."

Heath, who had only just finished writing his initials, looked up at her with a puzzled frown.

"Search for him?"

"Certainly, for of course, he must be in London," Miss Wynch remarked, quite calmly, as Heath began to understand what she meant. "If you will permit me, of course."

Heath nodded quickly, his heart swelling in his chest at how remarkable this lady was.

"You are a marvel, Miss Wynch, thinking about such things sooner than I would be able to consider them. I do not know where I shall begin, but yes, I would be very appreciative of your company. As I have said, you are the only one who knows the truth in all of its murkiness and if you so wish, if you still desire to be close to me then I would delight in having you by my side."

Miss Wynch took the dance card from him, her fingers brushing his.

"I am glad to hear it, Lord Landon." she murmured softly. "For that is precisely where I want to be."

CHAPTER TEN

"*L*ord Landon?" Bridget looked towards the gentleman who now held her heart. "There is something I must ask you."

The gentleman smiled down at her as they walked arm in arm through Hyde Park.

"But of course."

She cleared her throat.

"Might you consider asking Lady Yardley to assist you in your search for your brother?"

Lord Landon immediately frowned.

"You speak of 'The London Ledger.'"

"Yes, I do." Bridget squeezed his arm lightly. "It is something that can be easily done and in such a way, it will not be obvious as to why you seek your brother."

Lord Landon shook his head.

"Were I to write that I seek out my brother, that I should be grateful for any knowledge of where he is, I would not surprise many people. They would believe that my brother has taken himself away somewhere, and that I seek him to set to rights whatever wrongs he has done." His shoulders dropped, his head turned away from her. "It would not be the first time."

This last sentence was said with such a heavy sigh that Bridget knew at once that there was a great sadness in Lord Landon's personal relationship with his brother. Of course, she considered, it would be very difficult indeed to have a brother with such little regard for his own propriety, who cared so little for how the family name might be so damaged by his behavior.

"I hope that you know I will stand by your side even if the truth should come out, do you not?"

Lord Landon threw her a brief smile.

"Unless your father should forbid it."

Bridget did not allow herself to become so concerned, shaking her head.

"My father agreed to our courtship, did he not? He did so with such swiftness that I think even my mother was astonished."

Lord Landon chuckled, though his smile remained.

"It does not mean that he will continue to agree, should what I have done be discovered."

Bridget took a deep breath.

"In such a circumstance, I am certain that we would find a way." Her face grew hot at the sharp look which came to her, with Lord Landon possibly understanding what she meant. She lifted one shoulder in half shrug, choosing honesty over pretense. "After all, what would one scandal be on top of another?"

Much to her relief, Lord Landon laughed aloud.

"Are you truly so committed to me that you would consider eloping?"

Bridget smiled as she spoke.

"I have already declared myself quite determined to

stand by you, Lord Landon," she told him. "Do you truly think that such a thing would not be permissible for me?"

They had not spoken of marriage, but he had made himself clear as far as *his* intentions, and she now was making it plain that she had no desire to pull back from a gentleman who had stolen her heart. Even though his statement had shocked her, the truth he had told her revealed more of his character to her. The fact that he had been so honest was in his favor, and there *was* a way for him to shake some of the guilt from himself, by telling his brother the truth about what he had done. It seemed rather strange to Bridget's mind that Lord Barrett would be so determined to enact some sort of revenge so many years later, particularly when he had so far seemed so contented with the situation, but that was not for her to consider. All which was required of her was to aid Lord Landon in whatever way he sought to make amends and to promise him of her continued affection. She knew precisely the sort of gentleman he was now, his past no longer hidden.

"Has the confession of my misdeeds not driven you from me?"

"My heart has been a little bruised, certainly," she admitted, keeping her voice low so that only he could hear her. "But I have committed myself to you – if you should have me. That means, regardless of what takes place - even if my father should forbid me from doing so, I will find a way to be near you."

Lord Landon let out a heavy sigh.

"I do not think that I deserve someone such as you." His other hand settled on hers as they walked together. "I think you are a most extraordinary lady."

They walked in silence for some minutes. It was not a weighty silence, but one where they both simply rested within the quietness, their hearts seeming to beat together as one. Now that Lord Landon had told her the truth, there was no further barrier between them, and the awareness brought with it a sense of freedom that filled her heart. She lifted her chin, catching one or two glances being flung in her direction. Yes, she was walking arm in arm with Lord Landon, one of the most eligible gentlemen in London, and one who now had every intention, it seemed, of staying by her side forever. Of course, there came with that the heaviness of his past choices, and certainly, there were still consequences and difficulties to follow, but Bridget was determined that they could face such things together.

"I think it a wise idea to bring that to Lady Yardley." Lord Landon's brow furrowed. "I shall have to tell her all, of course, but I am not afraid of doing so." Squaring his shoulders, he smiled at her, chasing his frown away. "It seems as though, in telling you everything, I no longer have as much concern."

"I am glad to hear it. If you wish, we could go and speak with her this very afternoon?"

Lord Landon shook his head.

"Unfortunately, I cannot do so. I have promised Lord Atherton that I will meet him in White's for a short while." He rolled his eyes as Bridget laughed. "Although he is a very frustrating gentleman, he is also my friend. I have leaned on him heavily of late and he is a little concerned for me – as well being *entirely* interested in our connection! No doubt he will have a good many questions."

Laughing softly, Bridget pulled herself a little closer to him, their steps very slow indeed now.

"And shall you tell him, given his reputation for something of a loose tongue?"

Lord Landon grinned.

"I shall not hold anything back," he declared, making Bridget's heart fill with an even greater depth of affection. "I shall state that I am courting Miss Bridget Wynch, that I find her utterly delightful in all things, and that my heart is already entangled with hers."

Bridget allowed herself a happy, contented sigh as she smiled up into his eyes. With Lord Landon, she felt happier than she had ever been. She could not be sure of what was to come but, for the moment, she was very contented indeed.

MEANDERING SLOWLY BACK towards the carriage, walking a few steps behind her mother and her sister, Bridget smiled to herself, thinking about all that she had shared with Lord Landon. He had stepped away from her only a few minutes before, but Bridget had not wanted to walk with her sister, hearing Sophia complaining that Bridget was being courted before she was. When they had first come to Hyde Park, Sophia had remarked on Lord Landon's supposed change-ability, as though, in attending with Bridget, she hoped Lord Landon would not appear, Bridget's courtship would not begin and therefore she would find herself satisfied in her victory. Bridget had to admit to herself that there had been a slight sense of satisfaction in seeing Sophia's shoulders slump, the smile fading from her face as Lord Landon had stepped out of the carriage. Bridget's smile continued to linger as she thought of all that they had shared. Yes, there were still a few shadows but, with 'The London Ledger' and Lady Yardley's help, she was quite sure that they would be able to find Lord Barrett's whereabouts. Then there could be a discussion, an apology, and perhaps the whole matter could come to an end. Such a thought was, she considered, mayhap too much to hope for, but it was still within her. She still hoped, still dreamed, still wished - but no matter what came for Lord Landon, Bridget was quite determined to remain with him.

"Was that Lord Landon I saw you walking with?"

Bridget turned her head, her heart turning over in surprise at being so interrupted. A lady had come to walk with her, looking at her with piercing green eyes. Something about her was familiar, although Bridget could not recall her name.

"I do beg your pardon?" She lifted one eyebrow. "Forgive me, mayhap we have been introduced some time ago, but I am afraid I do not remember your name."

The lady shrugged.

"Do not concern yourself. I am not at all offended. Might I ask if it *was* Lord Landon you were walking with?"

Bridget blinked before she replied. Whoever this lady was, she was clearly familiar enough with Bridget that she felt able to ask such questions. With a small sigh, Bridget shrugged her shoulders. After all, everyone who had been walking in Hyde Park would have seen her on Lord Landon's arm, so it seemed foolish to try and hide it from this lady now.

"Yes, it was Lord Landon." She smiled quietly to herself. "I very much enjoyed my walk with him this afternoon."

"As well you should." The lady shook her head, and it was only then that Bridget realized she had not reminded Bridget of her name "However, Lord Landon is not a gentleman to be trifled with. He gives the appearance of being a fine, upstanding fellow, but I assure you he is not."

Considering this, Bridget did not feel any immediate

sense of alarm. The way the lady spoke, it appeared that she wanted to warn Bridget away from the gentleman which was something that Bridget had considered might occur. After all, the warnings in 'The London Ledger' would have been read by everyone, not just this lady. Clearly, having read what had been placed within the Ledger, she was now concerned for Bridget's reputation.

"I do not think that I have anything to be concerned about, but I thank you for your consideration." Speaking as firmly as she could, but keeping a smile on her lips, Bridget glanced across at the lady. "I appreciate your concern for me, however, but I do not believe that what was written in 'The London Ledger' about him is true."

"Ah, but I can assure that you that it is." The lady stopped suddenly, and much to Bridget's surprise, grasped her arm tightly, her fingers curling around her wrist, pulling her back so that she could not keep walking. "I can promise you that everything *I* say about Lord Landon is true also. He is not a gentleman who has any great kindness about him. He has made promises and then broken them – you *must* trust me on this matter."

Pulling her wrist away from the lady, and rather irritated by her overfamiliarity, Bridget lifted her chin.

"And I do not appreciate your warnings, nor your demand that I believe them." Keeping her voice steady, she took a step back, furthering the distance between them. "I will not be taken in. I will not believe that Lord Landon is as you might think him to be, based on nothing more than a rumor."

"You are not listening to me." Speaking even more fiercely now, the lady shook her head in obvious disbelief over Bridget's evident lack of trust in her words. "He has done a great wrong. He has injured others most severely.

There is a truth which he must keep back from all of us in the hope of preserving his otherwise pristine reputation."

Growing confused, Bridget took a steadying breath, glancing at her mother and sister who were still making their way toward the carriage.

"I must hurry after my mother."

She did not want to stay, did not want to linger to hear what else the lady might say about Lord Landon, particularly when she knew it would most likely be based on the rumors which had now been circulating for a couple of days.

"Again, you do not understand. It is to *me* that he has done all these things. It is I who have suffered."

In an instant, everything Bridget had intended - her intention to hurry after her mother, to leave this lady behind her, to forget everything which had been said – flew away from her. Looking back into the flashing eyes of the lady – a lady who was, she considered, not a good deal older than herself, Bridget allowed herself to consider what was being said.

"You say that Lord Landon has been the one to injure you?" The lady nodded her head. "I confess I find that very hard to believe."

None of this made any particular sense, for surely the person who had written this thing about Lord Landon in the Ledger was his brother, as they had considered! It would make sense for Lord Barrett to seek revenge over the stolen title, but who was this lady, then? Was she someone else that Lord Landon's brother had hired, so that she might go about London, warning young ladies away from the gentleman, telling them lies?

"I assure you it is true." The lady passed one hand over her eyes, shaking her head. "I understand that you may not believe me, but I assure you, I know Lord Landon better than you. The way he has pained me now makes me fear that he will do the same to you." Something began to beat hard and fast in Bridget's chest, as though those words had an air of truth about them. It was very faint but yet at the very same time, Bridget told herself, seemed most unlikely. "You would be best to stay away from that gentleman." The lady spoke fiercely as Bridget's heart began to tear itself into tiny pieces. "Believe me when I tell you - he is not worthy of you."

"I do not know what that means." Bridget threw up her hands. "I do not know what any of this means, precisely, or why you think I will simply believe your words because *you* have decided it is right for me to know them."

The lady threw her a flashing smile, which seemed quite out of place with the rest of the swirling tension that blew between them.

"A lady coming to tell another of what Lord Landon has done, in the hope of rescuing her from his clutches. *That* is what this is."

Trying to push away the growing friction by allowing herself a long breath, Bridget shook her head.

"I confess that I do not know who you are. I do not remember us ever being acquainted, but even if we have been, there is no reason for you now to come and insist that I believe whatever it is that you tell me about Lord Landon." Forcing boldness to the fore, she lifted her chin. "Understand this: whilst I appreciate your warnings, I will not be stepping away from him."

"Then on your own head be it." The smile faded, and the eyebrows crashed down as the lady threw up one hand, spinning on her heel to walk away. "Mayhap he will not break your heart as much as he broke mine."

Bridget stared after her, uncertain still as to who the lady was, and whether she could trust what her intentions had been, in coming to speak to her. What if this lady was, in fact, the person who had included the article in 'The London Ledger'? Was she in some way connected to Lord Landon's brother? But if she was, then surely she would have spoken of the title, and what Lord Landon had done? Instead, however, she had spoken of her own broken heart, of how Lord Landon had injured her so severely that she could no longer permit him to give his affections in any way to any other lady, without delivering a dire warning, with the intent of driving them apart.

Shaking her head at this, Bridget took in steadying breaths, watching as the lady walked away, her head held high. Quite why she had shown such perseverance was beyond Bridget, unless it was that it came from a place of deep concern, as she had said. Perhaps it *was* that the lady was worried about Bridget's connection to Lord Landon, but if that was so, then why had she simply forced herself upon Bridget? She had not once introduced herself, and even when Bridget had tried to ask, had not given her name. Was that not a little odd?

"I do not recognize her but, at the same time, I do."

Murmuring to herself, Bridget watched as the lady disappeared into the steadily growing crowd. She could not recall speaking with the lady before now, could not remember being introduced to her or even talking with her, before now, but there was something about her that remained familiar. Chewing on her lip, Bridget frowned, her head filled with heavy thoughts as she turned and made her way directly toward the carriage.

CHAPTER ELEVEN

"*And* so that is where I find myself, Lady Yardley."

Heaving a sigh, Heath looked first to Lady Yardley, and then turned his attention to Miss Wynch. She had been sitting quietly with a frown dancing across her forehead, ever since he had set foot into the house, some half an hour ago. Yes, he knew that she was concerned, but why she appeared so disturbed, he could not say. It was not as though she was hearing the story for the first time.

"That is quite a complicated situation indeed." Lady Yardley's voice was low, her expression rather heavy. "I know a little of your brother, Lord Landon. I confess, had I been in your position, I would have done much the same thing. After all, you are twins, and the matter of one being born only a few minutes after the other does not – to me – hold any particular strength as regards who should come first in line – despite what the law of primogeniture requires. It was wise of your father to hold back that information from you, and to educate both of you as if you were each the heir. It is a pity that the law does not take into account which of you would be better suited."

"Although he still, initially, had planned to admit that my brother had been born first." Heath shook his head. "And I still had to convince my father to burn the record which had been written at the time of our birth, naming my brother, and to keep the one which named me." Refusing to absolve himself of any responsibility, Heath grimaced. "I did not do the right thing, no matter how good my reasons for doing it."

Lady Yardley nodded slowly.

"Be that as it may, it is not something which I think you need feel too much guilt over. Especially given that," she continued quietly, "your brother, you said, shows no interest in having the title and seems rather glad that he has no pressing responsibilities."

"Yes, but I imagine that now, he has discovered what I have done, and therefore wishes to punish me for taking what could have been his." Heath dropped his hands into his lap. "He must be in London without my knowledge. He stated that he would be remaining at his estate this Season with his wife, but perhaps that is not what he is doing. Mayhap he has chosen to come to London and to punish me in the way that he deems fit."

"And you should like me to put into the Ledger that you are seeking an audience with your brother?" Lady Yardley began, only for Heath to shake his head.

"Not that I wish for an audience with him, only that I wish to know of his whereabouts."

Lady Yardley smiled at him.

"I am certain that I will be able to do something like that."

"There is one more possibility." Before Heath could say anything, Miss Wynch once again caught his attention, her voice troubled as she spoke. Her frown had lingered, driving a heavy groove into her forehead, her gaze darting between himself and Lady Yardley. It was clear that something severe was lingering in her thoughts, and Heath nodded encouragingly, wanting her to say more. "I had something of a strange encounter yesterday afternoon."

Heath blinked.

"An encounter?"

When she nodded and looked at him, something cold gripped Heath's heart. What else must he face now?

"It really was very odd." Miss Wynch shook her head as if trying to remember. "As I was walking away from you, Lord Landon, following my mother and sister, a lady came to walk beside me."

"A lady you recognized?"

Miss Wynch hesitated.

"That is the thing." She looked first at her cousin and then toward Heath. "I could not say whether or not I recognized her. There was something about her which was familiar, and she spoke to me as though we had been acquainted before, but try as I might, I could not recall her name, nor her title."

Lady Yardley let out a quiet chuckle.

"And one certainly does not want to ask in such situations," she remarked as Miss Wynch nodded in return. "That would not do. It would make us look most foolish."

"I confess that I did state, later in the conversation, that I did not remember her, but the lady did not appear too perturbed. She was much more interested in making certain that I was aware of her concern."

"Her concern." Heath echoed, now leaning forward in his chair, his tea forgotten as he settled his elbows on his knees, his hands gripped together. "Was her concern about me?"

Miss Wynch hesitated, then gave him a wry smile. "Yes."

"Then she has something to do with your brother." Lady Yardley made the connection very quickly indeed. "He is attempting to make certain that you have no enjoyment in this life whatsoever, so therefore sent a lady to speak to whoever it is that you have begun to draw close to."

Heath was about to agree, only for Miss Wynch to interrupt.

"Forgive me, but I do not think so."

Silence ticked through the room for a few seconds as she looked from one to the other of those present again. Fighting the urge to rise to his feet, to move across the room and sit directly beside Miss Wynch so that he might be near her as she spoke, Heath merely held her gaze.

"This lady warned you about Lord Landon?"

In answer to Lady Yardley's question, Miss Wynch nodded again.

"She said that Lord Landon would not treat me well, that he would break our connection without warning."

"I am not to be trusted then?" Heath pushed himself back in his chair. "This is the beginning of the consequences of which I was warned, I am sure. I am to be spoken of in such a way, even without my knowledge. Others will be told of my character so that those who are my acquaintances no longer wish to be so."

Miss Wynch's lips twisted as she shook her head.

"Again, I do not think that I would agree." The shadows grew darker across her face. "I do not think that this is related to your brother, Lord Landon. She expressed to me that you had been closely acquainted at one time and that, at some point, you had broken her heart." Her tongue darted out to lick her lips, an indication of the uncertainty

Heath considered she must now feel. "She sought to warn me, to pull me from your embrace before you could do anything to me as she said you had done to her."

"But that is foolishness!" Without warning, Heath found himself on his feet, his arms akimbo. "I have never once betrothed myself to any young lady, nor even courted, and I certainly would never endanger the reputation of a young lady! I am a gentleman who has, on occasion, had a kiss here, and an embrace there, but I can promise you that I have never been in any way seriously involved with a young lady! Everything I have done in the past, I have already explained to you, and there is nothing more to tell, Miss Wynch. I can *assure* you, there is nothing else for me to confess."

It was only when he finished speaking that Heath realized just how wide Miss Wynch's eyes had gone, astonishment radiating through her features. Taking a breath, he dropped his head to his hands, a little embarrassed at how sharply he'd spoken.

"I believe that I am convinced." It was Miss Wynch's soft voice that broke through the quiet, and as Heath lifted his head from his hands, he saw the tiny smile on her lips. "If you had allowed me to finish speaking, I would have promised you that I did not believe a word of what she said to me. Whatever this lady's intentions are, I am certain that she seeks only to injure you. Besides, I do not think that I could ever believe something so severe. There is no need to convince me of your truthfulness, Lord Landon."

Heath inclined his head, his voice quiet now.

"My apologies. I am perhaps a little overwhelmed by what was said to you."

"I understand." Miss Wynch smiled at him, her dark expression gone. "It is very confusing, but it is still a wise idea to write such a thing in the Ledger about your brother." Her shoulders lifted. "I suppose, I only suggest that, if you do find him, you consider the possibility that it may *not* be that he was the one who wrote such a thing about you."

"I can see that is sensible." Dropping back into his chair, he sent a quick look to Lady Yardley. She had been doing nothing but watching the scene play out, and now had a somewhat questioning look on her face. "Yes, Lady Yardley, include a message about my brother, as we had discussed. As for the lady who accosted Miss Wynch, I think that she must have made up the story out of some misplaced concern for you. That is all. We need not think of her again."

Lady Yardley nodded.

"Of course."

"And do you still intend to attend the evening soiree tomorrow, Miss Wynch? At Lord Atherton's home?"

"I am already looking forward to it – and to being in your company also." The warm smile brought great cheer to Heath's heart, and he returned it with one of his own. "And mayhap you and I might take a turn about Lady Yardley's gardens now before you take your leave?"

"I would be delighted." Catching Lady Yardley's small nod in his direction, he smiled at her, aware that he and Miss Wynch would only have a few minutes alone together, for propriety's sake. "I should like that very much."

Miss Wynch smiled, rose, and accepted his arm, with Heath leading her towards the door. They walked together out along the hallway and toward the gardens which Lady Yardley boasted at the back of the house. Looking down at her, Heath's heart swelled with both relief and great appreciation for the young lady he now carried on his arm.

"I do very much appreciate your faith in me, Miss Wynch."

Miss Wynch looked up at him in surprise.

"You do not think that, simply because a stranger tells me something about you, I will find myself suddenly confused as to my feelings, do you?" she asked gently. "I am a little stronger than that, Lord Landon."

"I can see that." Hoping he had not insulted her, he smiled warmly. "You have a quiet nature, but an inner strength. You may be quiet, but you are determined. That is something I greatly value."

Miss Wynch's smile lingered as they walked out into the gardens.

"I believe that you are the first to know me properly, Lord Landon – other than Lady Yardley and my friends, of course. I believe that my sister and my mother have always thought that I am nothing more than a quiet sort, unwilling to push myself forward - but the truth is, I have always been rather singular in my determination, albeit quiet about it."

"Something which I fully understand." As he looked down at her, appreciating her all the more, Heath's heart quickened. "In fact, I find you utterly breathtaking, Miss Wynch. I feel as though I do not deserve your company."

"That is nonsense," she laughed, her cheeks pink and her eyes a little softer. "It is about fate and good fortune, for it is that which has brought us together."

He shook his head.

"I would not agree entirely. Yes, fate may have brought us together, but it is your willingness to trust me which has furthered our connection. Many a young lady would have stepped back from me by now, and I cannot tell you how much I value you in that regard. The fact that you have been willing to step forward and to stay beside me, when many others would not have done, speaks very highly of you."

She smiled but said nothing and it was only then that Heath realized he had stopped their walk and turned to face her. He did not remember doing such a thing, but now they were standing so close together, his desire began to grow significantly. His hands were upon her, and she was the one who stepped closer now.

"Lord Landon."

Her voice was soft, her expression gentle, her eyes a little flared as she looked back at him. The expectation, and the hope were there, and try as he might, Heath could not resist the urge to pull her into his arms.

"I do believe that Lady Yardley would be a little irritated if she found me doing such a thing as this."

He spoke without thinking, seeing how she lifted her eyebrows at him.

"I think I should like it if you did not think of Lady Yardley at this moment." Her gentle teasing had him blushing, her hands creeping up to press lightly against his chest. "Surely you must know how eager I am for your company, for your nearness. It is not as though it is something I have hidden."

"And surely you must know how much I desire to be close to you in return."

His arms were around her now, as she spoke quietly, smiling up at him, and he was hardly able to believe what it was that she now offered.

"I do trust you, Landon." The way she spoke to him made his heart pound frantically in his chest, so great was his delight. "I do not think that I have ever desired anything more than to be in your arms."

There was something about this moment that was so entirely overwhelming that he could barely catch his breath. Her blue eyes sparkled vividly.

"I would not do such a thing if it were not for the fact that I have come to care for you so very much. My heart is already pulling towards you with every modicum of strength it possesses." Lifting one hand, he trailed it lightly across her cheek. "I am sorry for what happened with this lady and her approach to you. I wish that had not occurred, particularly when it appears that it is because of me."

"This matter shall be resolved." Her voice was even softer now, her breath shuddering as she let it out. "I have made my choice."

The significance of what she'd just said had Heath catching his breath.

"That you would choose me is almost incomprehensible," he answered quietly. "I truly think that."

Miss Wynch laughed softly, her eyes dancing as she leaned toward him.

"Regardless of your feelings, Lord Landon, I am afraid that you now have me and my heart to call your own." Her hands lifted up to his shoulders, her fingers wound around his neck, brushing the edges of his hair. Heath's heart beat so furiously that it was almost painful. When she looked at him, happiness evident in her smile, he could do nothing but respond.

"Bridget."

Speaking her name aloud seemed to bring him a fresh comprehension of exactly who it was he had in his arms. His astonishment over it grew as she tilted her face toward him. Heath could not resist dropping his head so that their lips finally met, brushing lightly against one another. It was more momentous than anything he had ever experienced before as if every part of him exploded with light and color. Certainly, he had stolen kisses now and again, but with Miss Wynch, the experience was all-consuming. Fire broke out in his lungs and at the same time, his breath was gone from him. Fighting to resist the desire to tilt his head to deepen the kiss. for fear it would overwhelm her, Heath forced himself to break the kiss instead. How much he wanted her to understand the depth of his affections! Recalling the fact that Lady Yardley might soon be standing nearby, Heath finally drew back. The way Miss Wynch sighed made him want to pull her all the closer, but he stopped himself in time.

"Aah…"

"I did promise Lady Yardley that I would be cautious – not in so many words, but by a look." He smiled as Miss Wynch frowned, clearly a little disappointed that their embrace was to come to an end. "But, this will not be the last of our kisses." He smiled at her as she blushed. "I can assure you of that."

"I am relieved to hear it." Her eyes twinkled up at him, and her cheeks were flushed. "There is nothing but joy when I am with you, Lord Landon."

She lifted her head again, and Heath could not help but drop another kiss on her lips. When she smiled, her eyes closed, and he had to fight not to pull her into his arms.

"This is where my happiness is to be found," he whispered gently. "With you, Miss Wynch. Only with you."

CHAPTER TWELVE

The evening soiree was a pleasant one, and yet, Bridget felt rather concerned. The Ledger had been published that very afternoon and, within it, the small article requesting information from anyone about the whereabouts of Lord Landon's brother. As she had come in, of course, Bridget had once more stepped into the shadows at the side of the room as her mother had led Sophia forward so that every gentleman might see her – but Bridget did not mind. From this perspective, she could look boldly around the room and be the first to see when Lord Landon arrived.

He had not set foot in the door as yet, which was a little unusual, given that she had been here for one full hour already. Lord Landon was not known to be tardy. Tilting her head, Bridget pushed away the slight niggle of concern that fought to blossom within her heart. Mayhap someone had already spoken to him about his brother, mayhap someone had come to call, wanting to tell him about what they knew, and this was now why he was late. She allowed herself a brief smile. Mayhap he would appear with a broad smile on his face, light in his eyes, and confidence in his step, telling her that he had managed to find his brother and now the matter could be brought to its conclusion.

"Miss Wynch."

Bridget turned her head swiftly as a familiar voice came to her.

"Lady Yardley."

Her friend smiled at her, although it was rather tight.

"You have read 'The London Ledger', I hope?" she asked, as Bridget smiled her reply. "I wrote as Lord Landon asked. Hopefully, we will find his brother again, very soon, and then all of Lord Landon's troubles will be gone."

Taking a breath, Bridget nodded slowly.

"Mayhap not all of them," she murmured quietly. "But a good many. I was thinking the very same thing."

Lady Yardley put a hand on her shoulder.

"The gentleman has you by his side. I am certain that whatever difficulties may yet face you, the fact that you have come to stand alongside him will mean a great deal." Bridget dropped her gaze a little, overwhelmed by the compliments Lady Yardley was offering her. "You still do not think as highly of yourself as you ought," her friend continued gently. "I do hope that you know how much of an asset you have been to Lord Landon. I do not think that he could quite believe that you are so willing to be alongside him. I believe he feared that you would turn your back upon him."

Bridget smiled.

"I could not have done such a thing. Everyone has made mistakes, have we not? I would not be wise to judge someone simply because of what he has done in the past. It is not something which I will ever say was good, but it *is* understandable."

"Certainly, it is. I would concur." Lady Yardley seemed about to say something more, only for Miss Middleton to come rushing towards them, her hands flapping.

"Good gracious, Miss Middleton, whatever is the matter?"

Lady Yardley caught her hand as the young lady came to join them.

"Lady Yardley." Her free hand reached out and caught Bridget's. "Is Lord Landon here this evening?"

Instantly, Bridget's heart began to quicken, such was the look in her friend's eyes.

"Not as yet, but I do believe that he intends to join us, though he is somewhat tardy. Why?"

Miss Middleton shook her head.

"It is the most peculiar thing," she replied quickly. "Give me a moment so I might bring Lord Hereford to join us." So saying, she stepped away and, after a few moments, came back to them with a fair-haired, hazel-eyed fellow who looked remarkably pleased to have Miss Millington tugging on his arm. "This is Lord Hereford." She gestured to the fellow as Bridget looked up at him, aware that Miss Middleton was speaking so quickly, that she did not intend to make the proper introductions. "We were only just discussing 'The London Ledger' and what had been written within it, and I happened to mention Lord Landon's brother – Lord Barrett Northdale, is it not?"

Lord Hereford inclined his head.

"Yes, that is so."

Miss Millington nodded, flinging out one hand in a dismissive gesture as though the fellow's name meant very little.

"I mentioned this to Lord Hereford, stating that Lord Landon was eager for news of his brother's whereabouts, only for Lord Hereford to laugh! I did not understand it at first but, well...." Turning, she gestured to Lord Hereford himself. "Come now, you must explain it."

Clearing his throat, Lord Hereford displayed a beatific smile, looking first to Bridget and then to Lady Yardley as though he were uncertain as to whom he ought to address this.

"I laughed – not in jest, you understand, but because I can assist Lord Landon very easily indeed!"

Bridget caught her breath, one hand going to her heart. "You mean to say that *you* know where Lord Barrett is at present? You have seen him?"

"I have, yes." Lord Hereford chuckled again though, as yet, Bridget could not understand why he did so. "Lord Landon cannot have looked very far, for his brother is contained within his own estate, a good distance from London!"

The surprise which flooded Bridget seemed to do the very same to Lady Yardley, for they both remained quite silent for some moments, each staring at Lord Hereford whose broad smile slowly began to fade.

"You – you mean to say Lord Barrett is not here in London?" Bridget could hear her voice, hoarse and quiet, struggling to be clear in her tone. "You are stating that he has not even left his estate?"

"No, he has not." Lord Hereford frowned now, rather than smiled, clearly aware that what he had said was of great significance. "I can assure you, Lord Barrett has not left his estate this last four months and more."

Lady Yardley took in an audible breath, one hand pressed lightly to her stomach.

"Might I ask how you can be so certain?"

Lord Hereford shrugged.

"Lord Barrett and I knew each other during our Eton days. He, of course, has no particular title beyond being 'Lord Barrett' simply because he is the son of an Earl, and I am only a lowly Baron – so thus, we fell in quite well together. We have remained friends, and I have often enjoyed his company over the last few years." Spreading out both hands, he lifted his shoulders again. "When I received an invitation to go to his estate and look over the plans for the improvements which are due to start very soon, I could not refuse! Even though it took me away from London for the first few weeks of the Season, it was an opportunity to reacquaint myself with my friend which I could not miss. Therefore, I made my way there and enjoyed his company immensely."

Swallowing at the tightness in her throat, Bridget pressed both lips tight together, then nodded.

"I see. And you have only just returned from his estate?"

"I certainly have. I made my way to London only last week, and this soiree is, in fact, one of the very first occasions I have attended." His eyes slid towards Miss Millington, who was now chewing her lip and completely oblivious to Lord Hereford's obvious interest. "I must say, I was very glad to be introduced to Miss Millington and to be of aid to you in this way. I assume that you are acquainted with Lord Landon, given your interest?"

Miss Millington turned back to Lord Hereford, forcing a smile.

"We are. Thank you for your aid, Lord Hereford. I look forward to dancing with you later this evening."

The gentleman blinked but then, with a brief smile,

nodded, inclined his head, and stepped away, understanding that the ladies now wished to talk among themselves. Miss Millington blew out a breath as she turned to face Bridget again, throwing up both hands.

"Lord Barrett was not in London, then."

Bridget's stomach did a little dance, but it was not a joyous one. Instead, it was one of confusion and apprehension.

"I do not understand. How can Lord Barrett not have been present in London at the time these things took place?"

"He did not have to be." Lady Yardley spoke slowly, although there was a frown on her face, betraying her confusion. "This could all have been arranged from his estate, I suppose. Even though Lord Hereford was present with him, it would not mean that he could not have made these arrangements. It would have taken a great deal of correspondence and certainly would be challenging to make certain that all went as he expected, but it is not an impossibility for him to have done so."

"But surely we must admit that such a thing would be a little unlikely?" Bridget shifted from one foot to the other as Lady Yardley hesitated. "It would be more than difficult, would it not? How would he even know of 'The London Ledger', let alone how to slip an extra page into it, as we suspected he had done?"

At this, Lady Yardley grimaced.

"Yes, you are right. It would be difficult, although not impossible. But this does make it more likely that someone else was to blame."

"Exactly. There is always the possibility that Lord Barrett is not guilty of what we suspect him of. What if he is *not* the fellow who has done all of these things to Lord Landon? What if it is someone else?"

Bridget turned her head, seeing that Lady Cassandra had come to join them when Bridget had not been aware of her presence.

"Cassandra. Lord Hereford, he –"

"Yes, yes, I know. I came to speak with you because I heard the very same." Lady Cassandra squeezed Bridget's hand. "I know that we are considering Lord Barrett to be the most likely person responsible for such things, but what if he is not?"

"Then I do not know what we are to do." For a moment, Bridget considered whether or not the gentleman had yet more dark secrets of which he had to absolve himself, but the thought was gone the next moment. She knew him well enough not to believe that. He had already told her of something which he swore he had never told another living soul. If he had trusted her with that, then there would be nothing he would not have told her. The lady she had spoken to popped into her mind, adding to her confusion. Taking a deep breath, she set her shoulders. "Let us hope that Lord Landon appears very soon. We will have to tell him of this news."

Lady Yardley sighed.

"This does cause a great deal of difficulty," she admitted, "for if there is no one to blame, then who precisely does Lord Landon think is attempting to cause him so much difficulty?" She turned and held Bridget's gaze. "And what is their motivation for doing so?"

~

"HE HAS NOT APPEARED."

Bridget swallowed hard as she shook her head. They had been present for almost three hours and, as yet, Lord Landon had still not arrived. It was very strange, for she had thought him to attend this evening's gathering, and had been looking forward to being in his company.

"Perhaps he has been held back by some business matter." Lady Cassandra offered her a comforting smile. "You need not look so concerned. I am sure that he will either appear very late, or you will have a note waiting for you when you return home."

Bridget tried to smile.

"I am sure that you are right." She could not quite keep the slight wobble from her voice but forced a smile to hide it. "I am sure that I am overly concerned when there is no need for me to be."

Her friend smiled softly.

"I understand your concern. As I have said, I am sure that there will be some simple explanation, however."

Accepting this, Bridget gestured to a nearby table, setting off to go and fetch herself a drink.

As she approached the refreshment table, a strong hand grasped her arm, and she turned quickly, expecting it to be Lady Yardley or Lady Cassandra, only to look into the fierce expression of the russet-haired, green-eyed lady she had met on one occasion already.

"Good evening." The hand still lingered on her arm, the lady's fingers sticking in rather painfully, and her voice, whilst soft, had a tone of anger. "You have decided *not* to stand away from Lord Landon then, as I suggested."

"I am more than capable of making my own decisions, I thank you." Bridget turned sharply so that the hand fell from her arm. "As I have said, I appreciate your concern but —"

"You *must* stay far from him." Rather than appearing in any way civil, the woman now seemed angry that Bridget had not done as she had suggested. "You are a stubborn, foolish creature but, then again, I suppose I should have expected that, given that Lord Landon has captured you with his *supposed* attention."

Entirely insulted, Bridget reared back. She could not even remember this lady's name, and yet here she was, insulting her for her choice to continue with her connection to Lord Landon.

You may be quiet, but you are determined.

Recalling Lord Landon's words to her, Bridget drew herself up.

"I do not know you. I am not acquainted with you, and the fact that you think you can speak to me in such a manner means that I do not *wish* to be acquainted with you." Her words were sharp, her tone severe, her eyes narrowed. "I do not believe what you have said about Lord Landon. I do not believe it for a moment. He has told me that it is untrue, and I am more inclined to believe his words than I am the words of a stranger."

To her utter astonishment, the lady threw her head back and laughed as though Bridget had said the most ridiculous thing she had ever heard.

"Oh, my dear child." Shaking her head, she patted Bridget's hand in an almost motherly fashion. "Of course you would say such a thing, and of course you would believe him. Why would you not?"

All the more irritated, Bridget lifted her chin.

"If you will excuse me."

She made to take her leave, only for the woman to catch her arm again, preventing her from stepping away. When she spoke this time, her voice was dark, her tone heavy.

"He has abandoned you this evening, has he not? He said that he would be here with you, but his absence is obvious. You will forgive him, no doubt, when he makes his excuses. You will tell him that it is quite all right, that you understand that the matter of business he had to deal with was quite necessary... and he will have captured you. He will have captured you entirely, and you will have no one to blame but yourself when the worst occurs."

Bridget drew herself up.

"I was not expecting Lord Landon here this evening."

The lie came quickly enough to her lips, but one quiet laugh from the lady told her that she was not believed.

"How very foolish you are." The statement had the lady herself turning away, throwing some final words over her shoulder. "Go. Find your Lord Landon and ask him where he was this evening. Whatever you do, however, do *not* go to his drawing room. Do not look up at the mantlepiece. Do not spy what is sitting there."

"What... What do you mean?"

Despite knowing that she ought not to ask a single question, Bridget could not help it and as she did so, the lady spun back towards her, the darkness in her eyes growing all the more.

"It will be your evidence, my dear, evidence that I speak the truth when I say that he is nothing but a liar. He is close to ruination, and you would be wise to remove yourself as far from him as you can."

Swallowing hard, Bridget held back any further questions she had. It would not be wise to ask them now, not when she was so confused in all that she thought and felt. How did this woman know what was on Lord Landon's mantlepiece in the drawing room? Surely, she could not know, not unless she had been there. Surely it could not be that Lord Landon had taken up with a previous connection at the very same time as declaring himself and his intentions towards her? Her heart cried out for her not to believe it, for her to continue to trust Lord Landon's words, but try as she might, what she had been told began to overwhelm her, to fill her with doubt.

"Are you quite all right?" Lady Yardley was suddenly next to her as the russet-haired lady stepped away. "She was the one who warned you at the first, in the park, I take it?"

Unable to speak, Bridget nodded.

"You must not believe her." Lady Yardley spoke confidently, but Bridget did not find the same within her own heart. "She is meddling, I am sure of it. Recall Lord Landon's difficulties, recall the threats he has been given. This is precisely what was meant by it, I am sure. Everyone's trust in him will be eroded until there is nothing more."

"Yes, I..." Bridget wanted to say that she would not believe it, that her trust would not be so quickly corroded, but the words simply would not come to her. Turning her head, she looked helplessly at Lady Yardley as her friend squeezed her hand sympathetically.

"I understand." With a deep breath, Bridget managed a small smile at Lady Yardley's words. "Do not fear. We will find the truth together – we will persist until it all becomes clear. Whatever you can hold on to, cling to it with all of your strength, Miss Wynch. Believe what you have seen with your eyes, and what you have heard with your ears, from Lord Landon. I do think that the gentleman can be trusted."

Bridget nodded slowly, still chewing over the thoughts which now ran through her mind. She wanted to tell Lady Yardley that yes, she had no difficulty in believing that Lord

Landon was everything he purported to be, but she could not. The shadow of doubt which lingered there held her fast, and even though Lady Yardley smiled encouragingly, waiting for her response, Bridget could give none.

Just what if it were true?

CHAPTER THIRTEEN

"My Lord." Heath looked up, then winced as the pain in his head came back with a vengeance. He had been forced to abandon his plans for stepping out the previous evening, given how severely his head had begun to ache - no doubt because of the great weight of difficulty which rested upon his mind. This morning, however, it was much improved, although the pain still lingered a little at the edges, ready to surge to the fore, as it had moments ago. "Forgive me, my Lord, for knocking again, but you did not answer."

Heath blinked.

"Did I not?" With a shake of his head, he let out a long breath. "I have not been quite myself today."

The butler gave no smile, but merely nodded his head, forever practical.

"I wished to inform you that Miss Wynch, Lady Yardley and Lady Cassandra have called upon you." He spread his hands. "I did mention that you are a little unwell, but said that I would ask whether you wished to see them."

Nodding quickly, Heath winced again.

"Yes, of course." He waved a hand. "Take them to the drawing room. I shall join them there in a moment. And send refreshments up to us at once."

Standing up straight and ignoring the flash of pain which shot through his head, Heath made his way to the looking glass, glancing at his reflection, and quickly resolving that his appearance was quite adequate. The ladies would have to simply put up with his pale face, the dark shadows beneath his eyes, and the slight disarray of his hair, given that he had not expected any guests. Why Miss Wynch had come calling so early in the day, he did not know, but he was glad that she had arrived, nonetheless. He had meant to write a note to her, informing her of why he had been absent the previous evening, but as yet he had been unable to do so. His head had only stopped paining him so severely a little over an hour ago.

Having lifted his brush from the side table, and run it over his hair a couple of times, hopefully improving his appearance, Heath took a deep breath, set his shoulders, and turned his feet to the door. Within a few moments, he was in the drawing room, stepping forward and greeting Miss Wynch with as much enthusiasm as he could manage. The sunshine which streamed through the window seemed a little brighter now that she was near him.

"Miss Wynch. How good to see you." Stepping forward, he reached for her hands. She gave them to him, but to his confusion she did not smile and rather turned her head away as he bowed over them. "I must apologize immediately for my lack of communication with you. I meant to come to the soiree last evening, but a most painful headache had me abed from very early. I could not even lift my head to give an instruction for a note to be sent to you."

Miss Wynch turned her head to look at him, but Heath,

remembering his duties, released her hands and greeted Lady Yardley and then Lady Cassandra. Gesturing for the three of them to sit, he chose to sit near Miss Wynch, still a little confused by the coldness which seemed to come from her.

"I hope that your head does not still pain you?"

Heath managed a small smile, pulling his attention from Miss Wynch to Lady Yardley.

"It is a little painful still, but not as terrible as it was last evening. With every hour that passes, it troubles me less." Again, he looked at Miss Wynch. Why was she looking so pale? Why was she refusing to look at him? Foreboding crept into the edges of his mind, and he struggled to shake himself free. "I am sorry if you were concerned for me, Miss Wynch."

"I *was* concerned." Finally, she spoke, but there was no warmth in her tone. "You said that you would be in attendance, and I did not hear from you in your absence."

"As I have said, I was unable to do anything other than lie in my bed." Aware that this made him sound rather weak, Heath cleared his throat. "This morning I had every intention of writing to you, only for you to arrive at my door. You cannot know how glad I am to see you." Unfortunately for him, Miss Wynch did not smile at this. Something was very wrong, but Heath did not know what it could be. Surely Miss Wynch was more of an understanding sort? She could not hold it against him that he had been absent from last evening's event because of his headache, surely? That was not the sort of person he knew her to be. "Did you... did you have a pleasant evening?" This question seemed to hang in the middle of the room as the three ladies looked at one another. Growing a little impatient, Heath threw up his hands. "Something is clearly troubling all of you. Whatever it is, might I ask you to tell me about it? I do not much like sitting here being all too aware that there is something wrong but having no understanding whatsoever of what it might be."

"Miss Wynch was spoken to, again, by the same lady she told you about, who had accosted her in the Park." Lady Yardley spoke briskly, and Heath sank back into his chair. "You can understand, I am sure, that she was a little upset by the conversation."

Heath closed his eyes, frustrated.

"Whatever was said to you, I am very sorry for it." Softening his tone, he turned to look at Miss Wynch again, and she gazed at him with rather sharp eyes. "Did she once again attempt to push you away from me?"

"Certainly she did." Miss Wynch lifted an eyebrow. "She also suggested that I might find something significant on your mantlepiece."

Blinking hard as confusion flooded him, Heath looked towards his mantlepiece, then back to Miss Wynch.

"You would find something on my mantlepiece?" he repeated, as Miss Wynch lifted an eyebrow. "I do not understand what you mean. How can I have something on my mantlepiece from this lady, if I do not know who she is?" Miss Wynch tilted her head and instantly, Heath understood what the concern was. Whatever the lady had said, she appeared to have made Miss Wynch doubt him... "Do you mean to say that you believe this person-"

"I confess that I do not know what to believe," Miss Wynch interrupted, her eyes now going towards the mantlepiece. "She stated that if you *did* have something on your mantlepiece in the drawing room, it would prove that what she had said to me about you was correct."

A tight knot formed in Heath's chest. Whoever this lady

was, she was attempting to pull Miss Wynch away from him as best she could. Her attempts were driving a deep and unrelenting fear into his heart, a fear that the lady would manage to do precisely as she intended.

"You cannot believe her." Swallowing hard, he rose to his feet, going directly towards his mantlepiece. "If there is something here then I..." To his utter horror, there was in fact, something present on his mantlepiece, something which he had not noticed before now. Reaching for it, he lifted it down, frowning in confusion as he held the silver brooch with a single diamond in the center. "I did not know that this was here."

His voice was a whisper. Heath looked directly at Miss Wynch, but her eyes were tight shut, her lips trembling. Horrified, Heath looked down at the brooch again. How had such a thing come to be here? And how had it not been found by any of the staff?

With sudden purpose, he turned and strode to the bellpull, tugging it hard. Within a few moments, the butler had arrived, and Heath practically pulled him into the room, gesturing to the three women.

"Pray inform Lady Yardley, Lady Cassandra and Miss Wynch what happened last evening."

The butler's face turned a little pink as he cleared his throat and clasped both hands behind his back.

"After dinner, his Lordship became unwell with a painful head. After about an hour of attempting to relieve it with a cold compress, his Lordship decided that it would be best to retire to bed. The physician was sent for. He came and offered a little laudanum to help ease the pain. Thereafter, his Lordship slept for the rest of the evening, and did not rise until late this morning."

Heath lifted his chin as Miss Wynch's eyes finally opened.

"If you wish, I can send for the physician also." There was a commanding tone to his voice which he had not meant to be there, but such was his eagerness to defend himself, he could not prevent it from springing forward. "I tell you no lies, Miss Wynch. That is *precisely* what occurred last evening."

Something like tears began to shimmer in Miss Wynch's eyes as she looked at him.

"Then how did this brooch appear on your mantelpiece?"

Heath could give no answer to this.

"That is the problem, Miss Wynch. I do not know. Last evening, I was in my bed. I do not know if there were any comings and goings, for I was given some laudanum to help me sleep, and thus I did." He looked to the butler. "Might I ask if anyone came to call?"

The butler paused for a moment then shook his head.

"There was only one difficulty, my Lord." A little surprised at this, Heath acknowledged it with a nod, gesturing for the man to continue. "It was nothing more than a street urchin." The butler hesitated. "I did not think it was a particularly serious matter, which is why I did not inform you of it this morning, my Lord."

"But of course. I am not angry with you about anything. I simply wish to understand what has occurred." Glancing at the ladies, Heath frowned hard, then turned his gaze back to his butler. "Did you say that there was a street urchin *within* the house?"

Clearing his throat, the butler inclined his head.

"A child ran through the servants' quarters, and up into the house. It took some time to find him, my Lord. He was hiding in one of the cupboards, having stolen some trinkets - no doubt hoping to wait until all were abed and make his escape. He was found and was quickly thrown from the house, the items he had purloined having been recovered from his person."

Heath scowled, turning back to Miss Wynch.

"It could be that this child placed the brooch where he was told to." He shrugged both shoulders, praying desperately that she would consider his suggestion. "I know that it does seem a little far-fetched, but I assure you that I had no visitor here last evening, I had no lady stepping into the house, and I certainly did not remove a brooch and place it on the mantlepiece."

Miss Wynch's eyes flooded and before Heath could say anything further, she had dropped her head and immediately began to sob. Dismissing the butler quickly, Heath practically threw the brooch down onto a small table, before rushing to Miss Wynch. Heedless of Lady Yardley and Lady Cassandra's presence, he bent down in front of her, and wrapped one arm around her shoulders, whispering to her that he was not angry with her over any of this. When she finally lifted her head and looked into his face, her eyes were still sparkling with tears.

"I am sorry, Landon."

"You need not be." His relief was so great, it was as if he had stepped outside on a winter's day, catching his breath with the chill. "Someone – no doubt, my brother - is attempting to ruin my reputation, to drive away those that I have come to care for. They are beginning with you, Miss Wynch. I have no doubt that they will continue with others."

Before he could say anything further, the door was

suddenly flung open, and Lord Atherton strode inside. Looking over his shoulder to the fellow, Heath arched one eyebrow, but Lord Atherton's face was a picture of fury. His eyes were wide, blazing with evident anger, his face hot, his stance a furious one as he flung out both hands - one to either side.

"You placed a bet about me in White's betting book?"

Heath slowly got to his feet, leaving one hand on Miss Wynch's shoulder.

"Whatever are you talking about?"

Lord Atherton was clearly enraged, throwing up both hands and storming towards Heath as though he were deliberately angering him all the more.

"You know exactly what it is that you have done." He drew closer, one finger pointing at Heath's chest. "How could you place such a bet about me? How could you do such a thing? I thought you were my friend."

"I *am* your friend." Remaining precisely where he was in the hope that Lord Atherton would not strike him, given there were ladies present in the room, Heath let out a slow breath, trying to contain his growing concern. "I assure you that I have had nothing to do with whatever it is you are talking about.

"And might we remind you, Lord Atherton, that someone is attempting to place a noose around Lord Landon's neck at present." Lady Yardley spoke mildly, but her calm voice appeared to be enough to stop Lord Atherton in his tracks. "You do know what I am speaking of, do you not?"

Pausing for a moment, Lord Atherton took a breath and turned to look in Lady Yardley's direction before his gaze shifted back to Heath.

"I did not know that you had spoken of it to anyone

else." A great breath rushed out of him, his shoulders slumping. "In truth, I had quite forgotten about that."

Breathing a good deal more easily, and greatly relieved that Lord Atherton had stopped without laying a hand upon him, Heath held up both hands.

"I assure you that I did not place any bet on you in White's," he swore. "If you recall, I have been threatened with consequences for some unspecified wrongdoing. It appears that it is not only you who has been under attack but also Miss Wynch."

He gestured to the lady and watched as Lord Atherton's eyes went to her. They rounded a little, and before Heath could explain further, Lord Atherton dropped into a chair, the fight now gone from him.

"Might I ask who it is that informed you about this bet?"

Lady Cassandra broke into the quiet as Lord Atherton's gaze swiveled towards her. He let out a long sigh, then shrugged both shoulders.

"A gentleman of my acquaintance, that is all." He shrugged again. "I did go to see White's betting book – and the bet *is* placed there."

"And what does the bet say?"

Making sure to keep his tone mild, Heath held his friend's gaze, seeing how Lord Atherton's shoulders rounded.

"It stated that I would be unable to..." His gaze roved around the room, heat building in his face. "Unable to become close to the widow Lady Phillips."

Lord Atherton's head dropped as Miss Wynch caught her breath, sending a flush of embarrassment into Heath's face.

"Atherton, I –"

"Yes, I know that you will tell me I ought not to speak so

in front of the ladies, but that is the truth of it. Now that I consider it calmly, however, I suppose it is not the sort of thing you would ever do. You would never write such a thing about me, even though I have embarrassed you on multiple occasions."

"No, I am not the sort of fellow who takes foolish revenge." Heath let out a wry laugh. "Though given the circumstances now, I may have to do so." This brought a little lightness to the conversation, and Heath nodded quickly to Lady Yardley's suggestion that another tea tray should be brought so that they might accommodate Lord Atherton also.

"There appears to be a good deal of difficulty surrounding me at present," Heath considered aloud as he again took his seat close to Miss Wynch, turning to face her. "I can assure you Miss Wynch - Bridget - I did not have anyone in this house last evening and I certainly did not have a lady present."

"I believe you." There was a slight wobble to Miss Wynch's voice. Her eyes glistened still with tears but her hand reaching for his was all the comfort Heath needed. "I am sorry that I was so easily convinced."

"You need not apologize." Heath's lips twisted, and frustration at all the pain this was causing filled him. "I might understand why my brother is doing such a thing but –"

"Only it cannot be your brother."

The sharp remark caught Heath unawares, a frown etching itself across his forehead.

"I beg your pardon?"

"It cannot be your brother," Miss Wynch repeated firmly. "Miss Millington spoke to us last evening, and she informed us that a gentleman by the name of Lord Hereford said that he was with your brother only last week, at your brother's country estate. Therefore, it cannot have been him."

Shock filled him as he stared at Miss Wynch, seeing her face go completely white. Taking a few moments to accept it, Heath sat forward, running both hands through his hair, and settling his elbows on his knees, looking down at the floor as he did so. Whatever did this mean? If it was not his brother, then who else could it be?

"I do not think that any of us can answer that." Realizing he had spoken aloud, answering his internal question, Heath looked up at his friend. "There is nothing else I have done, no one else I have injured," he protested, weakly. "I cannot think who else it might be, who would wish to do these things to me."

"But we have the lady who spoke to Bridget yesterday also," Lady Cassandra put in. "She is the only one we know of who is deliberately trying to push her away from you. Mayhap she is not a pawn, nor someone who has read the Ledger and now seeks to prevent Bridget from making a mistake, but rather the perpetrator."

Heath swallowed hard, lifting his head, and then straightening his spine.

"I suppose that must be a consideration. But what lady have I ever hurt?" His mind spun as he fought to find an answer. "I can think of no one!"

"Then mayhap you might tell Lord Landon of the appearance of the lady, Miss Wynch?"

Lady Yardley gestured to Miss Wynch, who nodded quickly, her face still rather pale.

"Certainly. As I have said before, I *do* recognize her, though I could not tell you where from." Her brow furrowed. "She is a little taller than me, although not by much. She has russet curls and lovely green eyes. All in all, she appears to be a very well-to-do lady, clearly of the same social status as us." Her frown grew heavier as she looked away. "I found her quite overpowering in her manner, for she spoke with great strength and firmness and did not seem to like it when I would not either do as she asked or believe what she stated." As she spoke, the memory of a face slowly began to swim in front of Heath's eyes. Reaching across, he grasped Miss Wynch's hand again, dragging air into tight, burning lungs. "Lord Landon?"

"Red curls? A long, straight nose, sharp cheeks, and firm jaw?"

His tone was heavy, and as he held Miss Wynch's gaze and saw her nod, Heath closed his eyes.

"Who is that you are thinking of?" Lord Atherton demanded quickly. "Come now, you must tell us the name of the person you are thinking of."

It was all so dreadful that Heath could not bring himself to speak. When he did, it was with an effort, pushing the words through bruised lips.

"It is not my brother." Air pushed from his strained chest. "It is his wife – my sister-in-law." He shook his head, threading his fingers through his hair, tugging at it lightly as though the gentle pain would bring him back to a sense of alertness. "Though that does not quite make sense, for she would have had to have been in London for many weeks now, to do this. I was certain that my brother said she was to be at the estate for the Season, not coming to town at all."

It was now Miss Wynch's turn to catch her breath, with one hand flying to her mouth as her eyes widened.

"I remember where I saw her!" Her words were coming more quickly now, tumbling over one another in her feverish excitement. "One day when I was going to the orphanage, my carriage collided with another. A lady was shouting at my driver and I spoke to her... And the woman I spoke to that day, that was her!"

Blinking rapidly, Heath felt a coldness send ice flooding through his heart, freezing his veins.

"Then she has been in London since my arrival." His voice was hoarse as Miss Wynch nodded. "Good gracious. It has nothing to do with my brother, then. All of this has had nothing to do with the title, nor with my father or his will and what we each inherited."

Struggling to take it in, he saw Lord Atherton close his eyes as he nodded slowly.

"It is from the hand of Mrs. Northdale, your brother's wife, that these threats have come?" Lady Yardley leaned forward in her chair with none of them noticing the maid who had stepped into the room to set down the tea tray. "Do you believe that she has done all of this?"

With a great sigh that lifted his shoulders, Heath nodded, remembering the fury which he had once seen in Mrs. Northdale's eyes.

"Yes, I believe that I am correct." Swallowing hard, he threw out his hands. "I imagine that she read the letter I sent to my brother before the Season, informing him that I intended to find a bride, and therefore decided to do all that she could to disrupt that."

"But why?"

Miss Wynch's eyes were wide.

"Because many years ago I refused to accept her." Heath shook his head, dropping his gaze from Miss Wynch. "We were acquainted before I took the title. Once my father had passed away, once I had finished my mourning period and returned to London, she pushed herself forward, and I did find her somewhat pleasing, but it was never with any intention for courtship or the like. We did not have such a serious connection as she desired. We did not court, we did not become betrothed. I recall her utter fury when she practically threw herself upon me, pleading a desperate affection - which I stated plainly that I did not return." A scowl formed. "Her supposed love faded into a furious anger that was almost overwhelming. In the weeks later, however, I heard that she was now being courted by my brother and, a short while later, they married."

Miss Wynch took in a shuddering breath.

"And that is why she is so determined to drive me from you." She reached out one hand, finally finding his again. "She does not want you to marry. She does not want you to have any sort of happiness. And if you do not marry, do not have a son to be your heir, then your brother is your heir. And should anything happen to you..."

"You are correct - I imagine she does not want me to marry. Perhaps she covets the title, as well as revenge, for surely it rankles that she is simply Mrs. Northdale, as Lord Barrett is a younger son, rather than being a Countess, as she would have been had he been Earl – or had she married me. She did threaten at the time that there would be consequences for my refusing her. I did not believe it, of course."

"Except that now it appears she has done as she promised." Lady Yardley murmured, the significance of her words sending a heavy weight down upon Heath's shoulders. "The only question now is what you are to do about it."

CHAPTER FOURTEEN

"*Y*ou may follow me."

Bridget, along with Lady Yardley, moved forward directly, following the butler as he took them to Mrs. Northdale's drawing room. Once she had learned the name of the lady, it had not been particularly difficult for Lady Yardley to find out where she lived and thus, a plan had been formed. Lady Yardley and Bridget had been uncertain as to whether or not they would be welcomed in, given that they were unexpected guests – but much to Bridget's relief, the lady appeared to be quite glad to have them visit.

Lady Yardley caught her gaze and smiled as they approached the drawing room, chasing away the wriggling nervousness which ran through Bridget's veins as they came to the door. With a breath, she settled her shoulders before walking inside, her eyes settling upon the lady who had done all she could to push her away from Lord Landon.

"So you have discovered me then."

Mrs. Northdale sat quietly in her chair, not rising to meet them, her hands clasped in her lap as her head tilted gently to one side. She no longer appeared to be the over-powering woman Bridget had met before. Now, she seemed almost demure, quiet, lacking in confidence. Her gaze darted from Bridget to Lady Yardley and back again.

"I have Lady Yardley to thank for that."

Casting Lady Yardley a quick look, Bridget allowed her gaze to move towards her maid for a moment, glad that she had taken a seat in the corner of the drawing room. It was a little unusual for Bridget to have her maid with her during afternoon calls, especially given that she was chaperoned by Lady Yardley, but much to Bridget's relief, Mrs. Northdale barely glanced at the girl, and certainly did not make any sort of remark.

"I do not think that we have ever been introduced, Lady Yardley." Mrs. Northdale's smile was delicate as she inclined her head. "I am glad to meet you."

Lady Yardley did not so much as blink.

"I do not think that you have ever been properly intro-duced to Miss Wynch either, Mrs. Northdale."

She arched one eyebrow while Bridget laced her fingers together to keep her from twisting them in an anxious manner. She had only this one opportunity and had to make certain that everything she said, every moment she spent in Mrs. Northdale's company, was carefully considered and controlled.

"Alas, we have not been." Mrs. Northdale settled one hand over her heart. "You are closely acquainted with Miss Wynch, I take it?"

"I am." Lady Yardley's chin lifted a little, no smile on her lips, and a somewhat fixed expression on her face. "Miss Wynch is a close friend of my cousin, Lady Cassandra, who is lately betrothed. Therefore, I have taken an interest in her also."

Mrs. Northdale nodded, although there was no smile on her face.

"I see." She waited for a moment as a tap came at the door, and called for the maid to enter with the tea tray. Gesturing for it to be set on the table before them all, she glanced at Bridget but then continued to speak to Lady Yardley, leaving Bridget to feel rather discomfited. "No doubt Miss Wynch has told you of my concern about Lord Landon?" Lady Yardley nodded, though she said nothing more, and Mrs. Northdale's gaze traveled once more to Bridget. "Are you to speak with me about him?"

"I have come to speak with you about what you have said about him." Bridget lifted her chin, making it sound, she hoped, as though she did not yet fully accept all that Mrs. Northdale had said. "Your words have spread some doubt into my mind."

Spreading out one hand towards Bridget, Mrs. Northdale sighed in evident sympathy.

"I am sorry to bring trouble to you, but Lord Landon is *not* a gentleman with whom you can trust your heart." Bridget rearranged her features into what she hoped was an expression of concern. "It is worrying for you, of course," Mrs. Northdale continued, perhaps spying Bridget's look. "But that is why I came to warn you. You must be on your guard against him."

Nodding slowly, Bridget did not say any word of agreement.

"As you may know," Lady Yardley broke in, her voice a little firmer now. "There have been some things written about Lord Landon in 'The London Ledger'."

Catching the way that Mrs. Northdale's eyes flashed towards Lady Yardley, Bridget allowed herself a secretive smile, hidden by the way that she lifted her cup of tea to her mouth. It was obvious to her that Mrs. Northdale knew precisely who Lady Yardley was, in relation to 'The London Ledger'.

"Yes, I am aware."

"There have also been some rumors spread about him," Bridget continued, picking up where Lady Yardley had left off. "His dear friend has recently come to him with some complaint, and these whispers written about him within 'The London Ledger' are most distressing."

"I can imagine that they are."

Picking up her teacup with delicate fingers, Mrs. Northdale again said nothing more, taking a sip of her tea as Bridget shared a quick glance with Lady Yardley.

"You are responsible for that."

Lady Yardley spoke again, her tone brooking no argument. Though she spoke with such confidence, Bridget's lungs caught her breath and held it captive as she fought the nervous anxiety which closed in on her. Mrs. Northdale looked first at Bridget and then at Lady Yardley before she eventually shrugged.

"If you are asking whether or not I organized someone to knock the papers from your hand so that another might be added to the pile, then yes, I will admit to it."

"Except that they were not knocked from *my* hands." Lady Yardley replied swiftly, and at that moment, the calm expression which had been so resolutely set on Mrs. Northdale's features finally began to shift. "It was Miss Wynch herself who took the papers to the publisher's office that day." Lady Yardley gestured to Bridget, who sat quite still. "This person you hired to do your bidding, did not *only* knock the papers from her hand. He also threw her against the wall where she knocked her head and injured her hand!"

Lady Yardley was being a good deal more severe in her description of what had occurred than Bridget might have been, but no doubt it was to encourage Mrs. Northdale's sympathy. From the way that Mrs. Northdale's eyes flared, Bridget believed it had done as was required.

"I am so terribly sorry, Miss Wynch." Mrs. Northdale finally set down her teacup, looking directly toward her. "The man I hired had been waiting there for several days for the arrival of the next publication. He obviously took his responsibilities seriously, perhaps driven by frustration at being forced to wait for so long." She smiled a slightly rueful smile, dropping her gaze to her hands. "I did have to pay him rather a great deal."

"It was a very upsetting experience." Bridget put a great deal of weight into her words, following Lady Yardley's lead. "It took me some time to recover."

Mrs. Northdale sighed and shook her head.

"I am truly very sorry. It was not at all my intention."

Bridget nodded.

"I understand that." Letting out a soft breath, she looked back to Mrs. Northdale, aware of how much she was searching her face. "You did all of this in an attempt to protect me from Lord Landon and his supposedly shadowy past."

Mrs. Northdale smiled, but it quickly faded as she sat a little further forward in her chair.

"Yes, I hope that you can see that."

"And what did you mean by what you wrote to be inserted into the Ledger?"

"You wish me to tell you my story? To explain it all?"

Bridget bit her lip, averting her eyes for a moment before taking in a deep breath, squaring her shoulders, and looking into Mrs. Northdale's face again. "Yes. I want to know."

"Very well." Mrs. Northdale sighed. "It is something of a sorrowful story and it pains me to tell it still – but I shall do so, for your sake."

"I thank you."

Mrs. Northdale settled one hand over her eyes for a moment, then began.

"Lord Landon and I were introduced before he took the title. We became closely acquainted, but his father became ill and thus, since it appeared that there might soon be a year of mourning likely to take place, he stated that he could not proceed to any closer acquaintance. I thought him most considerate." Bridget licked her lips, throwing a quick look towards Lady Yardley, who only narrowed her eyes a little as she watched Mrs. Northdale. Obviously, Lady Yardley had as much doubt about believing this story as there was within Bridget's heart. "As fate would have it, his father passed away and thereafter, he endured his time of mourning. Of course, I did all that I could to support him. I wrote notes whenever I could, thinking and praying for him often. When his time of mourning was at an end, you can imagine my delight in knowing that he would be in London for the Season. However, that delight soon turned to sorrow as he turned from me."

"But why?" Bridget widened her eyes a little, hoping that she appeared as fervent in her desire to understand as Mrs. Northdale might expect. "Why did he turn from you?"

Mrs. Northdale shook her head, a sad smile on her lips as she spread her hands wide.

"Because, my dear Miss Wynch, the title had changed him. He did not honor the promise he had given me."

Blinking rapidly, Bridget took a few moments to

consider what the lady had said, attempting to hide her disbelief and disdain from her expression. Mrs. Northdale was trying to ruin Lord Landon in Bridget's eyes, but she was not succeeding. Her words were false, her motivations cruel. Bridget had no doubt of that, meaning that everything which Mrs. Northdale said was greeted by a large amount of distrust. All the same, however, she had to give the appearance of belief, and thus she shook her head and pressed one hand to her eyes as though she could not believe what had been told her.

"It is almost too awful to believe."

Her voice wobbled as she dropped her hand and looked to Lady Yardley who nodded in a sympathetic fashion.

"You say that he did not honor the promise he had made you?" Lady Yardley asked as Mrs. Northdale nodded.

But was that a small flickering smile on her face? Was it a smile of triumph, believing that now she had won Bridget over?

"It is precisely as you say." Mrs. Northdale sighed very heavily indeed, dropping her gaze to her clasped hands. "Lord Landon rejected me. He told me that he had never made any such promise, and that I was a fool. How much I cried! I had held myself back from others, waiting for his return, only for him to pretend that there was nothing between us any longer." Silently considering this, Bridget did not dare look at Lady Yardley, for fear that she would do something foolish such as roll her eyes in obvious disbelief. Instead, she looked at the floor, her jaw tightening as Mrs. Northdale continued. "He refused to listen to my pleas, stating that there was nothing of consequence between us any longer. I was left broken-hearted and alone." She sniffed, pulling a handkerchief from her sleeve, and dabbing at her eyes. "Much to my relief, however, his brother took pity on me, seeing that my chances of matrimony were somewhat lessened, given that I had waited for Lord Landon. Thus, you now find me wed to Lord Barrett, who has, in fact, turned out to be a much better gentleman than Lord Landon could ever be."

Bridget could not help but lift her eyebrows at this. It was more astonishing than anything she had heard thus far, for to hear that Lord Barrett Northdale was considered a better gentleman than Lord Landon was surely utterly preposterous. Turning her head so that Mrs. Northdale would not catch her expression, she gave a discreet nod to her maid, who then disappeared from the room without causing so much as a glance from Mrs. Northdale.

"Might I ask what has brought you to London *this* season, Mrs. Northdale?" At this question from Lady Yardley, Mrs. Northdale merely lifted one eyebrow. "Lord Landon has been present in London for many a Season. Why is it that you have come to London this year? Was it solely to push Miss Wynch away from him?"

Mrs. Northdale smiled softly, gesturing towards Bridget.

"My husband received a note from Lord Landon, stating that he intended to seek out a bride," she answered, confirming all of Bridget's suspicions. "He has never said such a thing before, but once I heard of it, I made preparations to come to London immediately."

"Do you intend to do the same year after year?" Bridget could not help but ask. "Are you to make certain that he never marries?"

Something gleamed in Mrs. Northdale's eyes and Bridget's stomach tugged hard, a swell of revulsion rising within her.

"If I must." She offered her a thin-lipped smile. "As I

have said, his brother is far more worthy than he. If he must carry on the family line, if he must bear the title one day, then so be it. There could be no one else more worthy."

"I see now your reasons for doing this."

Even though Bridget had been expecting Lord Landon's arrival, given that she had sent the maid out to fetch him, she herself started in surprise when he stepped into the room. His gaze was fixed on Mrs. Northdale, who immediately rose to her feet, her hands flying to her hips.

"How dare you come into my house without invitation!"

"Your attempts to hide your presence from me have failed."

Lord Landon ignored her statement, coming to stand behind Bridget and settling one hand on her shoulder, which she immediately reached up to press with her own. Mrs. Northdale looked first at Bridget and then at Lord Landon, her face paling as though she now realized that her attempts to ruin Lord Landon had failed entirely.

"It seems as though you have tricked me, Miss Wynch." Mrs. Northdale's jaw jutted forward, her sharp green eyes fixing themselves to Bridget. "Lies do not become a young lady."

Before Bridget could respond, Lady Yardley let out something of a choked exclamation.

"That is a very fine thing to say, from someone who has done nothing but trick and deceive," she retorted as Bridget nodded fervently.

"You have lied to me," Bridget added, as Mrs. Northdale's gaze continued to narrow itself all the more. "You have told me untruths about Lord Landon. You have attempted to pull me away from him. You have lied about him – not just to me, but to others. No doubt you paid someone to place a false bet about Lord Atherton in White's betting book under Lord Landon's name, did you not? You paid another to threaten him with heavy consequences. You placed falsehoods within 'The London Ledger'... and all because Lord Landon refused to marry you."

Both to Bridget's relief and horror, Mrs. Northdale did not disagree with anything she had said. Instead, her chin lifted, and she fixed her gaze on Lord Landon.

"We were to be wed."

Lord Landon immediately shook his head.

"No, we were not. We were not even courting. That is what you wanted from me, what you hoped you would gain from our acquaintance, but it is not what I offered you."

His hand tightened a little on Bridget's shoulder and she turned her head, looking up at him for a moment with a small smile, hoping that he knew she did not believe a word of what Mrs. Northdale was saying.

"But I waited for you!" Mrs. Northdale threw up her hands. "I wanted us to become betrothed once you returned to society after your father's passing."

Lord Landon shook his head.

"I never once offered you that. Your anger and your frustration ought to be directed toward yourself, rather than to me. In your attempt at retribution, Mrs. Northdale, you have failed."

Swallowing hard, Bridget lifted her chin, a little cowed by the sheer anger in Mrs. Northdale's eyes.

"You wanted desperately to be married to a gentleman with a high title - such as the Earl of Landon," she murmured softly. "You wanted your children to bear a significant title. Is that why you have so much determination to push any fortunate young lady away from Lord Landon? You hope that, in doing so, he will never marry, will never produce an heir, and, in time, that you will gain what you have always hoped for?"

The lady did not answer her. Her expression remained exactly the same, but after some moments of them simply staring at each other, a tiny smile started to tug at the edges of her lips. Bridget's stomach dropped with a heavy weight. It was then that she knew precisely the sort of creature Mrs. Northdale was - subversive, manipulative, and cruel, determined to get what she wanted for herself, regardless of the consequences for others. Shaking her head, she pulled her gaze away, unwilling to look at her any longer.

"My brother does not know of this."

"Of course he does not." Mrs. Northdale's voice was filled with mockery. "Do you really think he would sanction my behavior? I know what is best for us, however, and thus I acted. Your brother has always stated that he is relieved that he does not have the title, but I have found myself wishing quite the opposite. He does not know what is best for him, as I said, so therefore, I had to act alone."

"No longer." Lord Landon spoke with such confidence that Bridget immediately began to breathe a little more easily. She did not know what he intended, but whatever it was, she had every hope that it would bring an end to Mrs. Northdale's plans. "Your husband - my brother - has already been sent for. He and I will discuss a great many matters, including this." Again, his fingers squeezed Bridget's shoulder, making her understand that he had every intention of speaking about what he had done all those years ago. "This is the end of things. I do not think that we will have any need to be in each other's company again." Lord Landon inclined his head a little, showing more respect than even Bridget could manage. "Good day, Mrs. Northdale."

Bridget rose, took Lord Landon's arm, and walked close

beside him as they left the room. The moment that the door closed, however, she turned herself into Lord Landon's arms and he held her close, with Lady Yardley standing a short distance away, her head turned from them.

"You cannot know my relief at this moment," she told him softly. "It is all at an end, is it not?"

"It is almost at an end," he told her, a gentle hand lifting her chin so that she looked into his eyes. "When my brother has arrived and when we have spoken, *then* I shall be free. Free to give you the entirety of my heart without anything holding me back." He smiled at her, his brown eyes searching hers. "Might you be patient with me for a little longer?"

Bridget smiled at him, her heart so full that she thought it might explode with both joy and relief.

"Of course, I will wait for you, Landon. I will wait for you forever if I must."

EPILOGUE

"*And* you say you are not in the least bit angry with me?"

Heath took in his brother's expression, searching it carefully to see if there was even a hint of dissatisfaction but instead, Barrett simply grinned.

"I swear to you, there is not." He shrugged both shoulders. "I have always told you that I dislike responsibility. I have a good deal of it already, given that father left me a small estate – but I should certainly not have been pleased should I have been given the title and the obligations which come with it!" The grin slowly began to crumble. "I am sorry that our father created the situation he did, with us not knowing from the start who would inherit the weight of the title. I am sure that he did it with the best intentions, but look at the consequences! How differently might we each have lived our lives, if we'd known? I am sorry, also, for what my wife has chosen to do. There have been some... difficulties in our connection of late. I will not go into particular detail, but needless to say, we are both as selfish, as conceited, and as arrogant as each other."

Heath ran one hand over his eyes. The burden of guilt, which had weighed so heavily upon him for so long finally lifted free, allowing him to breathe a little more deeply.

"I do not hold anything against your wife." Now he had been so easily forgiven, he was able to do the same. "I do not think that we will ever be able to be companionable, however."

Barrett laughed, though it was somewhat rueful. Rising to his feet, he strode across the room as Heath got to his.

"I will take her home. We have much to discuss." He held out one hand. "I did not think she would behave as she did. I am truly sorry."

Heath grasped his brother's hand. They were so similar in appearance, yet so different in character, but this was the first time that he had ever heard his brother speak with such severity. It seemed as though, finally, Barrett was taking the responsibilities he had with more seriousness than he had ever done before.

"I am sure that your estate will flourish, should you give it the time and care it needs."

His brother chuckled, that smile reappearing as he slapped Heath on the shoulder.

"I am sure it shall. I will admit that my consideration of things has changed somewhat. I need to improve many things, in my house and in my life, and I have every intention of doing so, both for the present and for the future. And I have you as my example."

His brother's embrace was a little unexpected, but Heath appreciated it, nonetheless. He watched as Barrett left the room, lifting one hand in farewell before sinking slowly back down into his chair.

"I am free."

The words broke from his lips, but he did not smile,

letting out a long breath instead. So, then, this was what it felt like to no longer bear the weight of shame and responsibility. His brother had forgiven him, having no qualms about what Heath had done, but seemingly relieved instead. All the same, forgiveness had been required for Heath to take a breath and begin his life over again.

His next thought was of Miss Wynch. How much he desired to see her, how much he longed to once more be in her company, so he might tell her of everything which had just taken place, everything which had been said to him. Considering his heart, he let out another audible breath.

I love her.

He smiled. He loved Miss Wynch so desperately, it could not be ignored. She was a part of him now, and should she ever remove herself, he would be left as a broken man.

"Miss Wynch, my Lord."

Heath practically flung himself from the chair as the very lady had been thinking of stepped into the room. He waited for Lady Yardley or even her mother to appear with her, but no one did. Her face flushed as she dropped her gaze, perhaps seeing his questioning look.

"I am to go to the orphanage," she explained, coming a little closer, only to stand with her hands clasped in front of her. "The carriage is waiting for me, but I knew that you would be speaking with your brother, and... I was so eager to find out whether or not all had gone well, that I could not help but stop by." She bit her bottom lip, lowering her head a little more. "I hope that you are not displeased."

"Displeased?"

Striding forward, Heath threw his arms around her waist, lifted her boldly, and twirled her gently around. Miss Wynch laughed, her arms around his neck as he set her down, her clear blue eyes looking back into his.

"I assume that all has gone well, then?"

"It is more wonderful than I could ever explain to you." He brushed a tendril from her cheek, marveling at the softness there. "I told Barrett everything, and he merely laughed. Laughed, can you imagine it?" Passing one hand over his eyes, he shook his head. "Needless to say, he has forgiven me, stating that I need not ever have concerned myself. He is still very glad that he did not have my father's title to bear and continues to state that he is glad I have taken it from him." Again, he shook his head, hardly daring to believe it. "Barrett told me that I did not require his forgiveness, but he gave it nonetheless."

Miss Wynch smiled, sighed, and lifted one hand to press it against his cheek.

"And now you are free."

His heart seemed to still in his chest with the significance of the moment. Nodding, he settled his hand against hers.

"Yes, I am free," he repeated quietly. "I have no guilt nor secret shame remaining. It is as though I have been carrying such a heavy burden for so long that I forgot quite what it was like to be without it!"

She laughed softly.

"I am so glad to hear of your joy."

"It comes from more than that," he promised, moving even closer to her, gazing down into her eyes. "You have shown me so much already, and I know that there is even more for me to learn from you – and I eagerly look forward to it. I want our life together to be one of generosity to all, to have a consideration of others, and the happy contentment which comes from sharing what we have. *You* are the one who has shown me the value of that, Bridget. Your kindness, your considerate heart, and gentle nature urge me to become a better gentleman than I am at present." Lifting her hand to his mouth, he kissed it gently. "Would that make you happy?"

Miss Wynch tilted her head, her lips curving in the gentle smile he loved so much.

"I am already *more* than happy. I am practically delirious!"

"I am glad to hear it," he answered, dropping his hand to her waist again. "I feel the very same – though I would not be this way if I did not have you, my dear Bridget."

Her smile blossomed even more.

"You will always have me, Landon."

Those words were the only invitation he needed. Her sweetness was overwhelming, and he lowered his head at once, sharing with her the deep affection within his heart. Their kiss was long and sweet and this time, he did not hold himself back, allowing this new, fresh understanding of love to express itself to her in his actions. He held her tight, held her close, one hand trailing up her back, the other around her waist as he tilted his head a little. When he lifted his head, eventually, she sighed against his lips as he drew back, seeing her eyes still closed and the smile on her lips.

"I love you, Bridget."

Her eyes opened and she lifted her hand to his face again.

"I love you too." There was no surprise in her voice or expression, but rather a hope and a happiness sending light all through her. "I love you deeply, with my whole heart, and I believe I always shall."

"Which is why I wish to marry you as soon as I can," he promised, as she smiled softly, her hands sliding around his neck again.

"And I look forward to that day, wishing it ever closer,"

she whispered. "For I will love you from this day until death do us part."

I LOVE HAPPY ENDINGS, don't you? I am glad (almost) everyone got what they wanted!

THE NEXT BOOK in the series is a friend to lovers story. I That is, if they can manage to finally talk to each other! love that trope, don't you? You can preorder it in the Kindle Store! The Earl's Unspoken Love

DID you miss the first book in the **Only for Love** series, The Heart of a Gentleman? Read ahead to check out a sneak peek!

MY DEAR READER

Thank you for reading and supporting my books! I hope this story brought you some escape from the real world into the always captivating Regency world. A good story, especially one with a happy ending, just brightens your day and makes you feel good! If you enjoyed the book, would you leave a review on Amazon? Reviews are always appreciated.

Below is a complete list of all my books! Why not click and see if one of them can keep you entertained for a few hours?

The Duke's Daughters Series
The Duke's Daughters: A Sweet Regency Romance Boxset
A Rogue for a Lady
My Restless Earl
Rescued by an Earl
In the Arms of an Earl
The Reluctant Marquess (Prequel)

A Smithfield Market Regency Romance
The Smithfield Market Romances: A Sweet Regency
Romance Boxset
The Rogue's Flower
Saved by the Scoundrel
Mending the Duke
The Baron's Malady

The Returned Lords of Grosvenor Square
The Returned Lords of Grosvenor Square: A Regency
Romance Boxset
The Waiting Bride
The Long Return
The Duke's Saving Grace
A New Home for the Duke

The Spinsters Guild
The Spinsters Guild: A Sweet Regency Romance Boxset
A New Beginning
The Disgraced Bride
A Gentleman's Revenge
A Foolish Wager
A Lord Undone

Convenient Arrangements
Convenient Arrangements: A Regency Romance
Collection
A Broken Betrothal
In Search of Love
Wed in Disgrace
Betrayal and Lies
A Past to Forget
Engaged to a Friend

Landon House
Landon House: A Regency Romance Boxset
Mistaken for a Rake
A Selfish Heart
A Love Unbroken
A Christmas Match
A Most Suitable Bride

An Expectation of Love

Second Chance Regency Romance
Second Chance Regency Romance Boxset
Loving the Scarred Soldier
Second Chance for Love
A Family of her Own
A Spinster No More

Soldiers and Sweethearts
To Trust a Viscount
Whispers of the Heart
Dare to Love a Marquess
Healing the Earl
A Lady's Brave Heart

Ladies on their Own: Governesses and Companions
Ladies on their Own Boxset
More Than a Companion
The Hidden Governess
The Companion and the Earl
More than a Governess
Protected by the Companion

Lost Fortunes, Found Love
A Viscount's Stolen Fortune
For Richer, For Poorer
Her Heart's Choice
A Dreadful Secret
Their Forgotten Love
His Convenient Match

Only for Love

The Heart of a Gentleman
A Lord or a Liar
The Earl's Unspoken Love

Christmas Stories
Love and Christmas Wishes: Three Regency Romance
Novellas
A Family for Christmas
Mistletoe Magic: A Regency Romance
Heart, Homes & Holidays: A Sweet Romance Anthology

Happy Reading!
All my love,
Rose

A SNEAK PEEK OF THE
HEART OF A GENTLEMAN

CHAPTER ONE

"Thank you again for sponsoring me through this Season." Lady Cassandra Chilton pressed her hands together tightly, a delighted smile spreading across her features as excitement quickened her heart. Having spent a few years in London, with the rest of her family, it was now finally her turn to come out into society. "I would not have been able to come to London had you not been so generous."

Norah, Lady Yardley smiled softly and slipped her arm through Cassandra's.

"I am just as glad as you to have you here, cousin." A small sigh slipped from her, and her expression was gentle. "It does not seem so long ago that I was here myself, to make my Come Out."

Cassandra's happiness faded just a little

"Your first marriage was not of great length, I recall." Pressing her lips together immediately, she winced, dropping her head, hugely embarrassed by her own forthrightness "Forgive me. I ought not to be speaking of such things."

Thankfully, Lady Yardley chuckled.

"You need not be so concerned, my dear. You are right to say that my first marriage was not of long duration, but I *have* found a great happiness since then - more than that, in fact. I have found a love which has brought me such wondrous contentment that I do not think I should ever have been able to live without it." At this, Cassandra found herself sighing softly, her eyes roving around the London streets as though they might land on the very gentleman who would thereafter bring her the same love, within her own heart, that her cousin spoke of. "But you must be cautious," her cousin continued. "There are many gentlemen in London – even more during the Season – and not *all* of them will seek the same sort of love match as you. Therefore, you must always be cautious, my dear."

A little surprised at this, Cassandra looked at her cousin as they walked along the London streets.

"I must be cautious?"

Her cousin nodded sagely.

"Yes, most careful, my dear. Society is not always as it appears. It can be a fickle friend." Lady Yardley glanced at Cassandra then quickly smiled - a smile which Cassandra did not immediately believe. "Pray, do not allow me to concern you, not when you have only just arrived in London!" She shook her head and let out an exasperated sigh, evidently directed towards herself. "No doubt you will have a wonderful Season. With so much to see and to enjoy, I am certain that these months will be delightful."

Cassandra allowed herself a small smile, her shoulders relaxing in gentle relief. She had always assumed that London society would be warm and welcoming and, whilst there was always the danger of scandal, that danger came only from young ladies or gentlemen choosing to behave improperly. Given that she was quite determined *not* to behave so, there could be no danger of scandal for her!

"I assure you, Norah, that I shall be impeccable in my behavior and in my speech. You need not concern yourself over that."

Lady Yardley touched her hand for a moment.

"I am sure that you shall. I have never once considered otherwise." She offered a quick smile. "But you will also learn a great deal about society and the gentlemen within it – and that will stand you in good stead."

Still not entirely certain, and pondering what her cousin meant, Cassandra found her thoughts turned in an entirely new direction when she saw someone she recognized. Miss Bridget Wynch was accompanied by another young lady who Cassandra knew, and with a slight squeal of excitement, she made to rush towards them – somehow managing to drag Lady Yardley with her. When Cassandra turned to apologize, her cousin laughingly disentangled herself and then urged Cassandra to continue to her friends. Cassandra did so without hesitation and, despite the fact it was in the middle of London, the three young ladies embraced each other openly, their voices high with excitement. Over the last few years, they had come to know each other as they had accompanied various elder siblings to London, alongside their parents. Now it was to be their turn and the joy of that made Cassandra's heart sing.

"You are here then, Cassandra." Lady Almeria grasped her hand tightly. "And you were so concerned that your father would not permit you to come."

"It was not that he was unwilling to permit me to attend, rather that he was concerned that he would be on the continent at the time," Cassandra explained. "In that regard, he was correct, for both my father *and* my mother have taken leave of England, and have gone to my father's properties on the continent. I am here, however, and stay now with my cousin." Turning, she gestured to Lady Yardley who was standing only a short distance away, a warm smile on her face. She did not move forward, as though she was unwilling to interrupt the conversation and, with a smile of gratitude, Cassandra turned back to her friends. "We are to make our first appearances in Society tomorrow." Stating this, she let out a slow breath. "How do you each feel?"

With a slight squeal, Miss Wynch closed her eyes and shuddered.

"Yes, we are, and I confess that I am quite terrified." Taking a breath, she pressed one hand to her heart. "I am very afraid that I will make a fool of myself in some way."

"As am I," Lady Almeria agreed. "I am afraid that I shall trip over my gown and fall face first in front of the most important people of the *ton*! Then what shall be said of me?"

"They will say that you may not be the most elegant young lady to dance with?" Cassandra suggested, as her friends giggled. "However, I am quite sure that you will have a great deal of poise – as you always do – and will be able to control your nerves quite easily. You will not so much as stumble."

"I thank you for your faith in me."

Lady Almeria let out a slow breath.

"Our other friends will be present also," Miss Wynch added. "How good it will be to see them again – both at our presentation and at the ball in the evening!"

Cassandra smiled at the thought of the ball, her stomach twisting gently with a touch of nervousness.

"I admit to being excited about our first ball also. I do

wonder which gentlemen we shall dance with." Lady Almeria swiveled her head around, looking at the many passersby before leaning forward a little more and dropping her voice low. "I am hopeful that one or two may become of significant interest to us."

Cassandra's smile fell.

"My cousin has warned me to be cautious when it comes to the gentlemen of London." Still a little disconcerted by what Lady Yardley had said to her, Cassandra gave her friends a small shrug. "I do not understand precisely what she meant, but there is something about the gentlemen of London of which we must be careful. My cousin has not explained to me precisely what that is as yet, but states that there is much I must learn. I confess to you, since we have all been in London before, for previous Seasons – albeit not for ourselves – I did not think that there would be a great deal for me to understand."

"I do not know what things Lady Yardley speaks of," Miss Wynch agreed, a small frown between her eyebrows now. "My elder sister did not have any difficulty with *her* husband. When they met, they were so delighted with each other they were wed within six weeks."

"I confess I know very little about Catherine's engagement and marriage," Lady Almeria replied, speaking of her elder sister who was some ten years her senior. "But I *do* know that Amanda had a little trouble, although I believe that came from the realization that she had to choose which gentleman was to be her suitor. She had *three* gentlemen eager to court her – all deserving gentlemen too – and therefore, she had some trouble in deciding who was best suited."

Cassandra frowned, her nose wrinkling.

"I could not say anything about my brother's marriage, but my sister did wait until her second Season before she accepted a gentleman's offer of courtship. She spoke very little to me of any difficulties, however - and therefore, I do not understand what my cousin means." A small sigh escaped her. "I do wish that my sister and I had been a little closer. She might have spoken to me of whatever difficulties she faced, whether they were large or small, but in truth, she said very little to me. Had she done so, then I might be already aware of whatever it is that Lady Yardley wishes to convey."

Miss Wynch put one hand on her arm.

"I am sure that we shall find out soon enough." She shrugged. "I do not think that you need to worry about it either, given that we have more than enough to think about! Maybe after our come out, Lady Yardley will tell you all."

Cassandra took a deep breath and let herself smile as the tension flooded out of her.

"Yes, you are right." Throwing a quick glance back towards her cousin, who was still standing nearby, she spread both hands. "Regardless of what is said, I am still determined to marry for love."

"As am I." Lady Almeria's lips tipped into a soft smile. "In fact, I think that all of us – our absent friends included – are determined to marry for love. Did we not all say so last Season, as we watched our sisters and brothers make their matches? I find myself just as resolved today as I was then. I do not think our desires a foolish endeavor."

Cassandra shook her head.

"Nor do I, although my brother would have a different opinion, given that he trumpeted how excellent a match he made with his new bride."

With a wry laugh, she tilted her head, and looked from one friend to the other.

"And my sister would have laughed at us for such a

suggestion, I confess," Lady Almeria agreed. "She states practicality to be the very best of situations, but I confess I dream of more."

"As do I." A slightly wistful expression came over Miss Wynch as she clasped both hands to her heart, her eyes closing for a moment. "I wish to know that a gentleman's heart is filled only with myself, rather than looking at me as though I am some acquisition suitable for his household."

Such a description made Cassandra shudder as she nodded fervently. To be chosen by a gentleman simply due to her father's title, or for her dowry, would be most displeasing. To Cassandra's mind, it would not bring any great happiness.

"Then I have a proposal." Cassandra held out her hands, one to each of her friends. "What say you we promise each other – here and now, that we shall *only* marry for love and shall support each other in our promises to do so? We can speak to our other friends and seek their agreement also."

Catching her breath, Lady Almeria nodded fervently, her smile spreading across her face.

"It sounds like a wonderful idea."

"I quite agree." Miss Wynch smiled back at her, reaching to grasp Cassandra's hand. "We shall speak to the others soon, I presume?"

"Yes, of course. We shall have a merry little band together and, in time, we are certain to have success." Cassandra sighed contentedly, the last flurries of tension going from her. "We will all find ourselves suitable matches with gentlemen to whom we can lose our hearts, knowing that their hearts love us in return."

As her friends smiled, Cassandra's heart began to soar. This Season was going to be an excellent one, she was sure.

Yes, she had her cousin's warnings, but she also had her friends' support in her quest to find a gentleman who would love her; a gentleman she would carry in her heart for all of her days. Surely such a fellow would not be so difficult to find?

CHAPTER TWO

"I should like to hear something... significant... about you this Season."

Jonathan rolled his eyes, knowing precisely what his mother expected. This was now his fourth Season in London and, as yet, he had not found himself a bride – much to his mother's chagrin, of course. On his part, it was quite deliberate and, although he had stated as much to his mother on various occasions, it did not seem to alter her attempts to encourage him toward matrimony.

"You are aware that you did not have to come to London with me, Mother?" Jonathan shrugged his shoulders. "If you had remained at home, then you would not have suffered as much concern, surely?"

"It is a legitimate concern, which I would suffer equally, no matter where I am!" his mother shot back fiercely. "You have not given me any expectation of a forthcoming marriage and I continually wonder and worry over the lack of an heir! You are the Marquess of Sherbourne! You have responsibilities!"

Jonathan scowled.

"Responsibilities I take seriously, Mother. However, I will not be forced into–"

"I have already heard whispers of your various entanglements during last Season. I can hardly imagine that this Season will be any better."

At this, Jonathan took a moment to gather himself, trying to control the fierce surge of anger now burning in his soul. When he spoke, it was with a quietness he could barely keep hold of.

"I assure you, such whispers have been greatly exaggerated. I am not a scoundrel."

He could tell immediately that this did not please his mother, for she shook her head and let out a harsh laugh.

"I do not believe that," she stated, her tone still fierce. "Especially when my *dear* friend, Lady Edmonds, tells me that you were attempting to entice her daughter into your arms!" Her eyes closed tight. "The fact that she is still willing to even be my friend is very generous indeed."

A slight pang of guilt edged into Jonathan's heart, but he ignored it with an easy shrug of his shoulders.

"Do you truly think that Lady Hannah was so unwilling? That I had to coerce her somehow?" Seeing how his mother pressed one hand to her mouth, he rolled his eyes for the second time. "It is the truth I tell you, Mother. Whether you wish to believe me or not, any rumors you have heard have been greatly exaggerated. For example, Lady Hannah was the one who came to seek *me* out, rather than it being me pursuing her."

His mother rose from her chair, her chin lifting and her face a little flushed.

"I will not believe that Lady Hannah, who is so delicate a creature, would even have *dreamt* of doing such a thing as that!"

"You very may very well not believe it, and that would not surprise me, given that everyone else holds much the same opinion." Spreading both hands, Jonathan let out a small sigh. "I may not be eager to wed, Mother, but I certainly am not a scoundrel or a rogue, as you appear to believe me to be."

His mother looked away, her hands planted on her hips, and Jonathan scowled, frustrated by his mother's lack of belief in his character. During last Season, he had been utterly astonished when Lady Hannah had come to speak with him directly, only to attempt to draw him into some sort of assignation. And she only in her first year out in Society as well! Jonathan had always kept far from those young ladies who were newly out – even, as in this case, from those who had been so very obvious in their eagerness. No doubt being a little upset by his lack of willingness, Lady Hannah had gone on to tell her mother a deliberate untruth about him, suggesting that *he* had been the one to try to negotiate something warm between them. And now, it seemed, his own mother believed that same thing. It was not the first time that such rumors had been spread about gentlemen – himself included and, on some occasions, Jonathan admitted, the rumors had come about because of his actions. But other whispers, such as this, were grossly unfair. Yet who would believe the word of a supposedly roguish gentleman over that of a young lady? There was, Jonathan considered, very little point in arguing.

"I will not go near Lady Hannah this Season, if that is what is concerning you." With a slight lift of his shoulders, Jonathan tried to smile at his mother, but only received an angry glare in return. "I assure you that I have no interest in Lady Hannah! She is not someone I would consider even stepping out with, were I given the opportunity." Protesting his innocence was futile, he knew, but yet the words kept coming. "I do not even think her overly handsome."

"Are you stating that she is ugly?"

Jonathan closed his eyes, stifling a groan. It seemed that he could say nothing which would bring his mother any satisfaction. The only thing to please her would be if he declared himself betrothed to a suitable young lady. At present, however, he had very little intention of doing anything of the sort. He was quite content with his life, such as it was. The time to continue the family line would come soon enough, but he could give it a few more years until he had to consider it.

"No, mother, Lady Hannah is not ugly." Seeing how her frown lifted just a little, he took his opportunity to escape. "Now, if you would excuse me, I have an afternoon tea to attend." His mother's eyebrows lifted with evident hope, but Jonathan immediately set her straight. "With Lord and Lady Yardley," he added, aware of how quickly her features slumped again. "I have no doubt that you will be a little frustrated by the fact that my ongoing friendship with Lord and Lady Yardley appears to be the most significant connection in my life, but he is a dear friend and his wife has become so also. Surely you can find no complaint there!" His mother sniffed and looked away, and Jonathan, believing now that there was very little he could say to even bring a smile to his mother's face, turned his steps towards the door. "Good afternoon, Mother."

So saying, he strode from the room, fully aware of the heavy weight of expectation that his mother continually placed upon his shoulders. He could not give her what she wanted, and her ongoing criticism was difficult to hear. She did not have proof of his connection to Lady Hannah but, all the same, thought poorly of him. She would criticize his close acquaintance with Lord and Lady Yardley also! His friendships were quickly thrown aside, as were his explanations and his pleadings of innocence - there was nothing he could say or do that would bring her even a hint of satisfaction, and Jonathan had no doubt that, during this Season, he would be a disappointment to her all over again.

"Good afternoon, Yardley."

His friend beamed at him, turning his head for a moment as he poured two measures of brandy into two separate glasses.

"Sherbourne! Good afternoon, do come in. It appears to be an excellent afternoon, does it not?"

Jonathan did so, his eyes on his friend, gesturing to the brandy on the table.

"It will more than excellent once you hand me the glass which I hope is mine."

Lord Yardley chuckled and obliged him.

"And yet, it seems as though you are troubled all the same," he remarked, as Jonathan took a sip of what he knew to be an excellent French brandy. "Come then, what troubles you this time?" Lifting an eyebrow, he grinned as Jonathan groaned aloud. "I am certain it will have something to do with your dear mother."

Letting out an exasperated breath, Jonathan gesticulated in the air as Lord Yardley took a seat opposite him.

"She wishes me to be just as you are." Jonathan took a small sip of his brandy. "Whereas I am less and less inclined to wed myself to *any* young lady who has her approval... simply because she will have my mother's approval!"

Lord Yardley chuckled and then took a sip from his

glass.

"That is difficult indeed! You are quite right to state that *you* will be the one to decide when you wed... so long as it is not simply because you are avoiding your responsibilities."

"I am keenly aware of my responsibilities, which is precisely *why* I avoid matrimony. I already have a great deal of demands on my time – I can only imagine that to add a wife to that burden would only increase it!"

"You are quite mistaken."

Jonathan chuckled darkly.

"You only say so because your wife is an exceptional lady. I think you one of the *few* gentlemen who finds themselves so blessed."

Lord Yardley shrugged.

"Then I must wonder if you believe the state of matrimony to be a death knell to a gentleman's heart. I can assure you it is quite the opposite."

"You say that only because you have found contentment," Jonathan shot back quickly. "There are many gentlemen who do not find themselves so comfortable."

Lord Yardley shrugged.

"There may be more than you know." He picked up his brandy glass again. "And if that is what you seek from your forthcoming marriage to whichever young lady you choose, then why do you not simply search for a suitable match, rather than doing very little other than entertain yourself throughout the Season? You could find a lady who would bring you a great deal of contentment, I am sure."

Resisting the urge to roll his eyes, Jonathan spread both hands, one still clutching his brandy, the other one empty.

"Because I do not feel the same urgency about the matter as my mother," he stated firmly. "When the time is right, I will find an excellent young lady who will fill my heart with such great affection that I will be unable to do anything but look into her eyes and find myself lost. *Then* I will know that she is the one I ought to wed. However, until that moment comes, I will continue on, just as I am at present." For a moment he thought that his friend would laugh at him, but much to his surprise, Lord Yardley simply nodded in agreement. There was not even a hint of a smile on his lips, but rather a gentle understanding in his eyes which spoke of acceptance of all that Jonathan had said. "Let us talk of something other than my present situation." Throwing back the rest of his brandy, and with a great and contented sigh, Jonathan set the glass back down on the table to his right. "Your other guests have not arrived as yet, I see. Are you hoping for a jovial afternoon?"

"A cheerful afternoon, certainly, although we will not be overwhelmed by too many guests today." Lord Yardley grinned. "It is a little unfortunate that I shall soon have to return to my estate." His smile faded a little. "I do not like the idea of being away from my wife, but there are many improvements taking place at the estate which must be overseen." His lips pulled to one side for a moment. "Besides which, my wife has her cousin to chaperone this Season."

"Her cousin?" Repeating this, Jonathan frowned as his friend nodded. "You did not mention this to me before."

"Did I not?" Lord Yardley replied mildly, waving one hand as though it did not matter. "Yes, my wife is to be chaperoning her cousin for the duration of the Season. The girl's parents are both on the continent, you understand, and given that she would not have much of a coming out otherwise, my wife thought it best to offer."

Jonathan tried to ignore the frustration within him at the fact that his friend would not be present for the Season, choosing instead to nod.

"How very kind of her. And what is the name of this cousin?"

"Lady Cassandra Chilton." Lord Yardley's gaze flew towards the door. "No doubt you will meet her this afternoon. I do not know what is taking them so long but, then again, I have never been a young lady about to make her first appearance in Society."

Jonathan blinked. Clearly this was more than just an afternoon tea. This Lady Cassandra would be present this afternoon so that she might become acquainted with a few of those within society. Why Lord Yardley had not told him about this before, Jonathan did not know – although it was very like his friend to forget about such details.

"Lady Cassandra is being presented this afternoon?"

His friend nodded.

"Yes, as we speak. I did offer to go with them, of course, but was informed she was already nervous enough, and would be quite contented with just my dear wife standing beside her."

Jonathan nodded and was about to make some remark about how difficult a moment it must be for a young lady to be presented to the Queen, only for the door to open and Lady Yardley herself to step inside.

"Ah, Lord Sherbourne. How delighted I am to see you."

With a genuine smile on her face, she waved at him to remain seated rather than attempt to get up to greet her.

"Good afternoon, Lady Yardley. I do hope the presentation went well?"

"Exceptionally well. Cassandra has just gone up to change out of her presentation gown – those gowns which the Queen requires are so outdated and uncomfortable! She will join us shortly."

The lady threw a broad smile in the direction of her

husband, who then rose immediately from his chair to go towards her. Taking her hands, he pressed a kiss to the back of one and then to the back of the other. It was a display of affection usually reserved only for private moments, but Jonathan was well used to such things between Lord and Lady Yardley. In many ways, he found it rather endearing.

"I am sure that Cassandra did very well with you beside her."

Lady Yardley smiled at her husband.

"She has a great deal of strength," she replied, quietly. "I find her quite remarkable. Indeed, I was proud to be there beside her."

"I have only just been hearing about your cousin, Lady Yardley. I do hope to be introduced to her very soon." Shifting in his chair, Jonathan waved his empty glass at Lord Yardley, who laughed but went in search of the brandy regardless. "You are sponsoring her through the Season, I understand."

His gaze now fixed itself on Lady Yardley, aware of that soft smile on her face.

"Yes, I am." Settling herself in her chair, she let out a small sigh as she did so. "I have no doubt that she will be a delight to society. She is young and beautiful and very well-considered, albeit a little naïve."

A slight frown caught Jonathan's forehead.

"Naïve?"

Lady Yardley nodded.

"Yes, just as every young lady new to society has been, and will be for years to come. She is quite certain that she will find herself hopelessly in love with the very best of a gentleman and that he will seek to marry her by the end of the Season."

"Such things do happen, my dear."

Lady Yardley laughed softly at Lord Yardley's remark, reaching across from her chair to grasp her husband's hand.

"I am not saying that they do not, only that my dear cousin thinks that all will be marvelously well for her in society and that the *ton* is a welcoming creature rather than one to be most cautious of. I, however, am much more on my guard. Not every gentleman who seeks her out will be looking to marry her. Not every gentleman who seeks her out will believe in the concept of love."

"Love?" Jonathan snorted, rolling his eyes to himself as both Lord and Lady Yardley turned their attention towards him. Flushing, he shrugged. "I suppose I would count myself as someone who does not believe such a thing to have any importance. I may not even believe in the concept!"

Lady Yardley's eyes opened wide.

"You mean to say that what Lord Yardley and I share is something you do not believe in?"

Blinking rapidly, Jonathan tried to explain, his chest suddenly tight.

"No, it is not that I do not believe it a meaningful connection which can be found between two people such as yourselves. It is that I personally have no interest in it. I have no intention of marrying someone simply because I find myself in love with them. In truth, I do not know if I am even capable of such a feeling."

"I can assure you that you are, whether or not you believe yourself to be."

Lord Yardley muttered his remark rather quietly and Jonathan took in a slow breath, praying that his friend would not start instructing him on the matter of love."

Lady Yardley smiled and gazed at Jonathan for some moments before taking a breath and continuing.

"All the same, I do want my cousin to be cautious, particularly during this evening's ball. I want her to understand that not every gentleman will be as she expects."

"I am sure such gentlemen will make that obvious all by themselves."

This brought a frown to Lady Yardley's features, but a chuckle came from Lord Yardley instead. Jonathan grinned, just as the door opened and a young lady stepped into the room, beckoned by Lady Yardley. A gentle smile softened her delicate features as she glanced around the room, her eyes finally lingering on Jonathan.

"I feel as though I have walked into something most mysterious since everyone stopped talking the moment I entered." One eyebrow arching, she smiled at him. "I do hope that someone will tell me what it is all about!"

Jonathan rose, as was polite, but his lips seemed no longer able to deliver speech. Even his breath seemed to have fixed itself inside his chest as he stared, his mouth ajar, at the beautiful young woman who had just walked in. Her skin was like alabaster, her lips a gentle pink, pulled into a soft smile as blue eyes sparkled back at him. He had nothing to say and everything to say at the very same time. Could this delightful young woman be Lady Yardley's cousin? And if she was, then why was no one introducing him?

"Allow me to introduce you." As though he had read his thoughts, Lord Yardley threw out one hand towards the young woman. "Might I present Lady Cassandra, daughter to the Earl of Holford. And this, Lady Cassandra, is my dear friend, the Marquess of Sherbourne. He is an excellent sort. You need have no fears with him."

Bowing quickly towards the young woman, Jonathan fought to find his breath.

"I certainly would not be so self-aggrandizing as to say

that I was 'an excellent sort', Lady Cassandra." he was somehow unable to draw his gaze away from her, and his heart leaped in his chest when she smiled all the more. "But I shall be the most excellent companion to you, should you require it, just as I am with Lord and Lady Yardley."

There was a breath of silence, and Jonathan cleared his throat, aware that he had just said more to her than he had ever said to any other young lady upon first making their acquaintance. Even Lord Yardley appeared to be a little surprised, for there was a blink, a smile and, after another long pause, the conversation continued. Lady Yardley gestured for her cousin to come and sit beside her, and the young lady obliged. Jonathan finally managed to drag his eyes away to another part of the room, only just becoming aware of how frantically his heart was beating. Everything he had just said to his friend regarding what would occur should he ever meet a young lady who stole his attention in an instant came back to him. Had he meant those words?

Giving himself a slight shake, Jonathan settled back into his chair, lost in thought as conversation flowed around the room. This was nothing more than an instant attraction, the swift kick of desire which would be gone within a few hours. There was nothing of any seriousness in such a swift response, he told himself. He had nothing to concern himself with and thus, he tried to insert himself back into the conversation just as quickly as he could.

Oh, no, Jonathan likes her! Perhaps he will have to change his mind about becoming leg-shackled! Check out the rest of story in the Kindle Store The Heart of a Gentleman

JOIN MY MAILING LIST

Sign up for my newsletter to stay up to date on new releases, contests, giveaways, freebies, and deals!

Free book with signup!

Monthly Facebook Giveaways! Books and Amazon gift cards!
Join me on Facebook: https://www.facebook.com/rosepearsonauthor

Website: www.RosePearsonAuthor.com

Follow me on Goodreads: Author Page

Printed in Great Britain
by Amazon